THE DARK ANGELS

The Dark Angels

François Mauriac

C L U N Y

Providence, Rhode Island

Cluny Media edition, 2018

For more information regarding this title
or any other Cluny Media publication,
please write to info@clunymedia.com, or to
Cluny Media, P.O. Box 1664, Providence, RI, 02901

WWW.CLUNYMEDIA.COM

Translation by Gerard Hopkins

Printed by permission

Library of Congress Control Number: 2018966255

ISBN: 978-1949899726

Cover design by Clarke & Clarke
Cover image: Vincent van Gogh, *Man Digging*,
1882, oil on paper
Courtesy of Wikimedia Commons

PROLOGUE

I fully realize, my reverend sir, that the mere thought of me fills you with horror. No word has ever passed between us, but you know me, or think you know me, because you were once the spiritual director of my cousin, Mathilde Desbats.... But please don't run away with the idea that I mind. As a matter of fact, you are the only man in the whole world to whom I should like to speak frankly. I remember the look on your face when I passed you in the hall at Liogeats on the occasion of my last visit to the home of my youth. You have the eyes of a child (how old *are* you?—at a rough guess, I should say about twenty-six), of a completely innocent child, though God has given you the power to know precisely to what depths a man's depravity can sink. But don't misunderstand me. It is not at all because of the clothes you wear, and of what they imply, that I feel the need to justify myself in your eyes. I take not the slightest interest in you as a priest. It is merely that I feel convinced that you, and you alone, are capable of understanding me. As I said before, you are a child—I would go even further, and say—a very young child, but a child with the gift

1

of wisdom. And I know, too, that your position as one who is "set apart" has been threatened.

There you are, then. Before so much as breathing a word about my own concerns, I have given you an exact statement of the opinion I formed of your character during the few moments in which I was able to study you when we met in Liogeats—in that squalid curé of souls where you live the life of a martyred priest, tied to the stake in a world inhabited by barbarous countryfolk.... But don't be afraid. I am very far from believing the current scandals. I am, my dear sir, extremely clear-sighted. Little though my knowledge of you amounts to, I can read your heart like an open book. As soon as I knew you had brought your sister to live with you at Liogeats, I realized, my poor, dear innocent, what you'd have to go through. It didn't take me long to recognize Tota Revaux. I had seen her about often, with her husband, in Montparnasse and Montmartre.... As a matter of fact, I once danced with her, without knowing who she was. I confess to having felt some surprise when I learned that you had taken that woman with the dyed hair and the plucked eyebrows into your house, after her marriage had been broken up. But I very soon realized that you still regard her with the blind devotion of a younger brother. But your half-witted parishioners are convinced that you are trying to pull the wool over their eyes. They say that she isn't your sister at all. Even in our own family circle, my cousin Mathilde, and her daughter Catherine, your one-time penitents, have put you on the Index. They now trudge all the way to Lugdunos when they want to make their confession. Good creatures though they are, they repeat all the filthy gossisp about you. Not that they really believe a word of it. You can well imagine the long faces they pull when they murmur with a sigh—"*Of course*, there's nothing *wrong*..."

Perhaps they have an obscure feeling that you are—how shall I put it?—capable of understanding that craving for the gutter which is so constant an element in the make-up of some people.... Don't be annoyed. Though I am up to my eyes in mud, though I am little better than a lifeless corpse, while you, upheld by the deep water, scarcely touch with your feet the white caps of the angry breakers, I dare swear you will not show the least surprise at the way in which my life has developed. For years now I have longed for just such a confidant as you, for a man combining the qualities of angel and brother. There is no barrier between us. Neither your virtue nor my guilt separates us: not even your habit—which I came within an ace of wearing myself—not even your faith.

I shall try to carry sincerity to the utmost limits without giving the angel in you the least excuse for tearing up what I have written. I shall be relentless in self-criticism; I shall avoid any pretense of establishing a moral alibi. My sole object is to convey to your understanding what can never be put into words.

If you have ever had occasion to hear a confession embracing the events of a whole life, you have not, I am sure, remained content with a dry catalogue of sins. You have striven to get a general view of your penitent's whole destiny, have traced the contours of its uplands, and shone the beam of your intelligence into the darkest recesses of its valleys. Well, then, here am I, a man who demands of you no gift of absolution, who has no belief in your power to remit sins, a man without the faintest shadow of hope. All the same, I am about to admit you to the most secret corners of myself. Don't be afraid—and this is most important—don't be afraid that what I am about to say will be for you a cause of scandal. Much in my story will strengthen your faith in that invisible world which it is your life's work to serve. The way into the supernatural often starts in the depths.

I don't want you to think that I belong by right of birth to the ranks of the bourgeoisie. It was my marriage that gave me the entrée to the great house at Liogeats. My father was the Péloueyres' bailiff, a former tenant-farmer, a man of keen intelligence, but quite uneducated. My mother died when I was eighteen months old. I am very like her. She was fair-skinned and exquisite. She and my father were the products of quite distinct races.... I believe that I know things about her which were long concealed from me. When a man has fallen very low, he feels the need to fix responsibility on one or other of his forebears. People of my sort hold very strongly that it is impossible to account for human degradation by the accidents of one poor devil's temperament; that only a downward movement starting from far back can have set going in him the rhythm of deterioration. In us, and through us, a host of men long dead and gone find satisfaction. In us and through us ancestral passions are released. Can we ever know how many of the shadowy dead push us along the path we hesitate to take? (But, you will say, can we ever know how many hold us back, how many help us in our struggle with the armies of darkness? To which I can only answer that our experiences, yours and mine, in this matter differ considerably!)

The dominating influence in my life took form while I

was still very young. As far back as I can remember, people liked me—or, more precisely, they liked my looks, and it was of my looks that I took advantage. You will not, I hope, suspect me of being the victim of a stupid vanity; I say all this simply in order to stress the causes of my apparent success and of my eventual undoing. But of this you must judge for yourself. My face, now that I am close on fifty, is, in essentials, the same face that led women to stop and kiss me on my way home from school. Today, my hair is white, but its silver sheen serves but to throw into relief the healthy tan of my complexion. My weight has not increased by a pound in the course of the last twenty years. I am still wearing suits and overcoats that I bought as a young man in London.

From my earliest years I have had what I can only describe as a gift of cold inquisitiveness. I was curious about this power of mine to charm, and enjoyed watching the effect it had on others. At first instinctively, later with increasing awareness, I strove to make use of it for my own purposes. This began, as I have said, when I was very young. Once, in that room at the Institution which stank of disinfectant— how well I remember that summer's morning!—the teaching Sister suddenly called us to order by rapping the desk with her ruler, and said very loudly, as the door opened: "Stand up, children, and show your respect for your benefactress." To the accompaniment of much scraping of benches, an old lady, wearing the kind of lace bonnet that one sees in portraits of Queen Victoria, entered the room. Hard on her heels appeared the Superior and one of the Sisters, both of them cooing and fluttering about her like a couple of doves, and apparently suffering the last extremities of uncontrollable laughter as the result of something said by the old lady which we had not caught.

"Hold out your hands!" said our form-mistress. In each of the grubby little paws our benefactress deposited three tiny sweets, one white, one pink, and one blue.

"So this," said old Madame Péloueyre, putting her knobbly hand on my head (she was the mother of old Jérome Péloueyre whom you buried last year), "this is the Gradère boy."

"And as intelligent as he is pretty," remarked the good Sister. "Gabriel, let our benefactress hear how well you can say your 'I believe in God...'"

I recited the Creed, speaking each word clearly and distinctly, and keeping my eyes fixed, all the time, on the old lady's face. It was then, I think, that I realized, for the first time, what effect they were capable of producing. She gave me an extra sweet.

"All Heaven is in that child's face." She held a murmured colloquy with the two Sisters. I heard the Superior say:

"Monsieur le curé would like to have him trained for the priesthood. He's a quiet, gentle lad, but still very young.... It would cost a lot of money, of course."

"I would gladly look after that side of it.... Nothing can be decided until after he has been confirmed. We will see then whether he has a vocation.... I don't want to take him out of his social class and leave him without roots...."

From then on I became extremely pious, and served the daily Mass. In the catechism class I was held up as a shining example. Nor would it be true to say that I was merely playing a part. I was easily moved by the Church liturgy. The lights, the chants, the smell of incense were my form of luxury. Greedily I took it all in, for it provided just that element of mysterious sumptuousness for which, though I did not know it at the time, my whole being hungered. When I compare the man I have become, my dear Abbé, with the devout little boy I was then, I can't help feeling that you priests are rather too indulgent to the outward signs of piety. Not only do they prove nothing: in certain cases, and with certain people, they are the signs of a deep-seated evil. Though the relations between Church and State were, at that time, decidedly strained, my father did finally give his consent to my embarking on the priestly profession. But it was only with the greatest difficulty that his objections were overcome. Parents, as a rule, want to see their children rise in the world…and I find it hard to explain his strange attitude to me at that time. What made him stand in the way of my advancement was, I think, a species of jealousy. He detested the thought of my future superiority. At thirteen I was apprenticed to a blacksmith. My muscles were still too undeveloped to make it possible for me to lift the great sledgehammer without a good deal of bodily contortion, and I was frequently beaten.

Not long before, my elder sister had died of consumption, worn out by hard work and ill-usage. She had been hired out by my father, while still a child, to some tenant-farmers as a maid of all work, which meant that she was at the beck and call of everybody, of animals as well as humans.

At long last he yielded to the representations of the curé and the ladies of the Du Buch family. As soon as the former was out of earshot, he said to me: "Better put yourself under instruction: you needn't take any final decision yet…"

I began by being one of the most brilliant pupils at the Seminary, and, without any doubt, I was the most popular. But why should a little country lout like me, a "learner" in a manual trade, who bore upon his body the marks of many a beating, have been so susceptible to the squalor of which the whole place was redolent? Are you familiar with the house in which the Péloueyres' present bailiff lives? It is very much as it was fifty years ago. I had spent my earliest years, before the blacksmith interlude, in conditions of physical neglect, due to the fact that I had no mother to take care of me. I ought, by rights, to have found the food served to us at the Seminary delicious. How came it, then, that I turned up my nose at it like any little spoilt scion of the bourgeoisie?

It so happened that, though I had been constantly in and out of the Péloueyre house, where I was regarded very much in the light of a tame cat, I had very seldom got beyond the kitchen. Things in the Du Buch house were very different. I was given the freedom of the drawing room and was frequently taken on their knees by the two ladies of the place. At the end of the last century, that house, to which the people of Liogeats always refer as "The Chateau," looked precisely as it does today. It stands a hundred yards back from the road on the outskirts of the little town, and is surrounded by pine trees. A great sweep of waterlogged grassland comes right up to the front steps, and the great trees of Frontenac close the view. At the time of which I am speaking, it was inhabited by the two old Du Buch ladies whom you never knew. They were sisters, one of them a widow, the other separated from her husband. The eldest of them had a daughter, Adila, who was a girl of eighteen when I was twelve. The younger also had a daughter, a few years my junior, called Mathilde, who later married Symphorien Desbats. During the holidays, these two cousins, Adila and Mathilde, were constantly at loggerheads about me. The elder wanted to read to me and to correct my exercises, while the younger, Mathilde, was forever at me to share her games. I must have been a very odd child! At first I showed a strong preference for my well-meaning and self-appointed governess, though she kept my nose to the grindstone with scarcely a pause. I had, I don't deny it, a very active mind. I was full of a natural curiosity, and was eager to absorb all the information I could pick up. No amount of mental work put me off. But from the age of fifteen, I began to be attracted to Adila for quite other reasons. She wouldn't have been bad-looking but for a pair of prominent eyes like a frog's, a thick-lipped mouth which was always half open, revealing a set of irregular teeth, and a heavy mass of hair which she wore piled on top of her head. But her worst feature was her neck, or, rather, absence of neck, for it was scarcely visible at all. Her face rose straight from her shoulders. She always looked as though she were bursting out of her clothes. Arms, legs, and figure, all seemed outsize and shapeless. Nevertheless, I began to find her rather pleasing. You must have noticed how, quite often, young, well-built, country lads have a way of marrying the most frightful women. They do so in response to the prompting of simple animal instincts, and these instincts were, during the years of my adolescence, strong in me. When, later, Adila Du Buch became my wife, people would have laughed in my face had I ventured to say that I had ever been in love with her. But I am speaking no more than the truth when I tell you that I did once find her distinctly alluring.... But what weakness I may have had for her was never sufficiently strong to keep me faithful.

You must forgive me for leading you by this roundabout way to the source of all my future destiny, or, rather (because I've got to go back still further), to the point in my life at which I began to go wrong with my eyes open, and with a concentrated awareness which you may find it hard to credit. Adila Du Buch was an extremely pious and charitable young woman, akin in temperament to Eugénie de Guérin. She clothed the poor, tended the sick, laid out the dead. She was moved, in particular, by a great sense of compassion for the old who, at that time, were left very much to their own devices in our part of the world, being, not seldom, positively victimized.... She would go visiting all over the countryside, driving her own trap, and always swathed in a red flannel cloak with a hood. She adored me. I was her one and only vice. For a long time she took delight in mothering me, and, in term-time, would make the trip into Bordeaux for the sole purpose of seeing me. Hampers of cold meats and sweets used to reach me from Liogeats. I will spare you the tale of how, from year to year, I grew more and more cunning at her expense. Moral depravity, carried to such lengths in one so young, cannot but give cause for wonder, and yet I am not sure that it is really very unusual. Many adolescents take a normal pleasure in stirring up mud, but the remarkable thing in my case was that I had not the slightest difficulty in persuading her of my utter innocence; that, where I was concerned, her suspicions were never once aroused.

Now, just imagine the terrible crises of conscience that may occur in the mind of a pious young female who holds herself to be responsible, not only for her own feelings, but for those, too, which she may rouse in the child committed to her care. And not just any child, mark you, but a budding seminarian, a future Levite! How came it that I could follow with so eager a curiosity the progress of a conflagration which I myself had started? None of Adila's pitiable little struggles escaped my notice, none of the excuses which she produced for always being absent from Liogeats when the Christmas and Easter holidays took me back there. She would make a retreat in some neighboring convent, but I almost always managed to prevail on her to return before I had to leave again for Bordeaux. Nor was I taken in for a single moment by the scruples of doubt which she produced as a reason for absenting herself from the Sacraments. What really was monstrous was that I could thoroughly enjoy the drama of the whole thing. My face never looked so innocent as during those years. In the crowd of grubby little seminarians I flourished like a lily. "Young Gradère?—a positive little angel...." Had I been a believing Christian, I should say now that every time I made my confession, every time I took communion, I was guilty of sacrilege. But I had already lost my faith.... And without faith, am I not right, it is impossible to commit sacrilege?

I had not even the excuse—I won't say of love (that goes without saying), but even of that initial attraction which, in my case, quickly died away. Not that I was incapable of falling in love. No, the fact was that with every passing year I found Mathilde increasingly alluring, and confided my feeling for her, with a deliberate assumption of simple-mindedness, to Adila. It wasn't enough for the poor girl to be harassed by scruples: jealousy poured oil on the flames—a jealousy which filled her with feelings of shame and horror. I think that at this time she would have been glad to die. Perhaps she should have died, perhaps that would have been the best way out of the situation—but I ought not to say a thing like that to you! She longed for death, and I wanted her to die. Had she done so, would not everyone have said that I was the cause? Certainly, I was convinced of it myself.... Adila ought to have killed herself, in spite of her faith, in spite of her fear of hell.... But all she did was to pray. She never stopped praying: even when she was in a state of sin she went on praying.... It is fortunate that the world laughs at old women's prayers. It is better that it should not know what power resides in them....

I got my *baccalauréate* just before I turned seventeen. About that time Combes was dealing devastating blows at the Church in France. Suddenly, I began to entertain grave doubts of my vocation. Not only did the curé of Liogeats and the Du Buch ladies refrain from uttering a single word of reproach, they actually decided to shoulder the cost of sending me to the University, where I was very anxious to pursue my studies. During those last holidays I hardly ever left the chateau. I took all my meals there. Adila no longer looked young. She was becoming fat and asthmatic. The way in which she continually kept a watchful eye on Mathilde and me became intolerably irksome. We did, however, manage to get free of it on occasion, because the poor girl was forever being called to this or that house in the parish. She began to see through my little game, but continued to regard me as her creation and her responsibility. Not for a moment would it have occurred to her that she had any right to upbraid me, no matter how lightly. At Bordeaux, I enrolled myself in the Faculty of Letters. From my patrons I received just enough to cover board and lodging. I had dreamed of leading a free and happy existence, but fact was very different from fancy, and I found myself, with practically no resources, living in a wretched room in the Rue Lambert, situated in the Meriadeck quarter of the city. I thought it only natural that Adila should help me, but she was allowed only the barest minimum of pocket-money, which meant that what she did send me had to be taken from her charitable funds.

I must, as I proceed with my story, be fair to myself and not disguise such extenuating circumstances as there may have been. No one realizes how terribly an eighteen-year-old student, with no family behind him, can suffer from cold and hunger. A protitute who lived in the same house took pity on me. Her name was Aline. Occasionally, we used to exchange a few words on the stairs. Then I got influenza and she looked after me. That was how the whole affair started. She noted down every penny she spent, but I never had enough money to be able to free myself from being dependent on her. She was very young and had not yet lost her freshness. The proprietor of a bar fell for her, and set her up in one of those little single-story houses which we, in Bordeaux, call "lean-to's." There was no concierge, and, consequently, little fear of indiscreet talk. The place was down in the docks, opposite a timber-yard.

I spent some part of each day there: the rest of my time I gave to frequenting the city library, where everything was grist to my mill (what didn't I read in those days?). In the evenings I used to go to the café which faces the Grand-Theatre. To me it seemed the most luxurious spot in the whole world. An orchestra used to play selections from *Werther* and *La Berceuse de Jocelyn*. After those first weeks of deprivation I was left with a craving for hot food and strong drink. Later, I learned—I won't say to feel ashamed, but to know what a man feels when it is always the woman who "stands treat." This situation lasted until the spring. One day, the proprietor of the bar whom I have already mentioned caught us. He had been warned by an anonymous letter. He forgave Aline, but I was slung out on my ear after a thrashing, the marks of which I carried about with me for a very long time.

I should like to cut the story short. But I must tell you everything, and this I shall do in the dry, factual style of a police report, avoiding undue emphasis, lest you be tempted, from sheer disgust, to throw what I have written into the waste-paper basket. The Easter holidays saw me back at Liogeats. Mathilde, now an orphan, was finishing her education at a school in Brighton, I spent all my time alone with Adila. All I want is that you should understand precisely the nature of my guilt. It is one thing to lead a young girl wrong, another to set about deliberately corrupting her. After my departure, Adila, who had once been so frank, went out of her way to lie and to find excuses for going into Bordeaux with the object of bringing me money. I made her pay dearly for her devotion, but, in spite of everything I could say, she obstinately refused to claim her share of the paternal fortune. By this time she knew me thoroughly: in fact, she was the only person who really did know me, and she played her hand cleverly. Poor, fat Adila! At Liogeats she avoided everybody. Madame Du Buch spent her days in lamentations, and was forever praying that Adila might "recover her faith." But on this point of the family inheritance the girl was as obstinate as a mule. Nothing that I could say would extract from her a promise to claim the money which her mother was keeping back without a shadow of justification. I had, at times, to ride her on a pretty light rein, so afraid was I that she might give me the slip altogether.

Truth to tell, though I had reduced her to a pretty low moral ebb, she was not yet in a mood of despair; and no matter how many crimes a Christian may have on his conscience, they don't, so long as he never despairs—I am right in this, am I not?—build between him and God any wall that a word or a sigh of contrition cannot demolish. This I knew, and knew, too, that she was waiting until I should be called up for my military service, was, indeed, counting on the inevitable separation that that would entail.

"I shall *have* to give you up then," she would say. "I shall go and hide myself, not in a convent but in the pig-sty belonging to some convent, or, better still, in a House of Penitents."

"Nonsense," I answered: "no matter how far away I may be stationed, you'll hunt me out, and…"

But I won't set down on paper the words I used. It was as though they had no connection with me.

I had a presentiment that I should never actually do my military service. I have had such presentiments in my life and they have always been proved true. What I knew would happen did happen. At the age of twenty I went down with pleurisy. I was never in danger, but the effects lasted a long time, and in this way I was saved from an army life. About that time I lost my father. Each year, just before the holidays, I solemnly announced to my benefactors a whole series of purely imaginary successes in University examinations, though, as a matter of fact, I never managed to get so much as an honorable mention. There were no other young men from Liogeats on the Faculty Class Lists, and it was easy for me to play that particular little game without any danger of being shown up.

At this time, too, I felt that my influence over Adila was so strong that I could safely threaten to abandon her unless she consented to do something about the money that was her due. She had finally broken with her family, and was living alone at Bilbao. I had no idea that she was pregnant. The poor girl had contrived this breach so as to have her child somewhere abroad. It was easy now for me to manage without any further assistance from her. Aline had written to tell me that her café proprietor was dead, and that she was free. I never knew whether he had made over part of his fortune to her during his lifetime, nor whether she had helped the processes of nature. I very foolishly adopted a policy of complete silence about the whole business. I say foolishly, because at that time she was quite unsuspecting, and might have blown the gaff. Later, when I came to realize how much to my interest it was to keep a tight hold on her, she was already on the defensive, and I could get nothing out of her.

I found her ensconced in a world of middle-class respectability, with a servant and an apartment of her own, living the life of a lady of leisure. She sub-let a room on the third floor to me, but I made use of it only on infrequent occasions. I paid her no rent. She had become a businesswoman, and had an interest in a number of—well, let us just say, "houses." Don't be alarmed: I shall pass quickly over this period of my life. All you need to know is that I became her professional associate, and took my share of the profits. This, more than any incident of my life, demands only the sketchiest of references. Do not avert your eyes, my reverend sir, unless you want to be turned into a pillar of salt. Aline had a genius for blackmail. It is a dangerous game, but we had a number of friends in the police force, which is why, as a matter of fact, we had to close down. They were altogether too greedy, and ended by killing the geese that laid the golden eggs.

Meanwhile, in January of 1913, Adila, the only living creature who really knew me through and through (which was probably why she adopted towards me an attitude of pitying comprehension that positively froze my blood), Adila wrote to tell me of the birth of our son, Andrès. She mentioned marriage, and did all she could to get her mother's approval. But by this time the old lady was in a very bad way, and died shortly afterwards.

But so long as I could live in the lap of luxury with Aline, I refused to consider the idea of such a marriage, magnificent though it would have been from my point of view. The thought of living with Adila filled me with horror. True, I was deeply attached to her, but whenever we were together I felt myself oppressed by a sense of shame which I find it impossible to describe in words. And that was strange in view of the depths of degradation to which I had sunk. I could not rid myself of the vision of what she once had been, a plump, healthy, happy Liogeats girl, doing her duty to her God, and beloved of all the poor for miles around; a girl whom I had dragged down though never driven to despair. She had never despaired.

Only later, when the war had already been raging for some time, did we get married. My hand was to some extent forced. I had, you see, to find some way of escaping from a situation which offered no other way out. A Medical Board had passed me unfit for service, and, at the beginning of 1915, I had gone to Paris with Aline. At first we made a lot of money, though I am not quite brazen enough to tell you how. Never had the trade in drugs been so flourishing. A lot of cocaine was coming into the country from Germany via Holland. All you need know, in order to understand the sequel, is that certain incidents, which might have had very unpleasant results, made it quite impossible for me to break away from Aline. After 1915 she had a stranglehold on me. Gone were the days when, in her besotted affection, she had nursed me in a room in the Rue Lambert of the Meriadeck quarter. She wasn't even the shrewd "Madame" who had taken me into partnership. Drink had always been her particular vice, and, as time went on, she sank deeper and deeper into the mire. She reached a point at which she no longer bothered about the ordinary affairs of life. She left them all to me. I swear to you that she had me exactly where she wanted me. For that you must take my word, and will not, I hope, insist on details.

To sum up: At that time there was a woman in my life— there still is—who spent her life lying in bed with a bottle of Pernod and a glass beside her, reading detective novels. She had given up washing altogether, and nobody kept the house clean. I won't try to describe to you the state of her embroidered sheets and silk nightdresses all torn and covered with stains. There were dirty glasses and empty bottles every-where.... She insisted on my going to see her on certain fixed days. She had made a proper fool of me, my dear sir. Nevertheless, I had been promised, something inside me told me that I had been promised (you will think I am quite mad!), that everything would go right for me in this world. And it is true that, in some ways, everything had gone right for me, that I have lived the life of a privileged person. At a time when so many young men of my age were suffering and dying in the mud of the trenches, I was snug and safe, and making money. "But it's not my fault," said a voice within me, "if you've got yourself into a jam with two women. Marry the rich one, and you won't have to bother any more about the other, who is poor and has a hold on you.…" I am perfectly well aware that when a voice speaks like that it is one's own.

I sent Adila a short letter in which I said that I had made up my mind to marry her. I left Paris round about Easter. I have a vivid memory of the evening on which I arrived at Liogeats. No one was expecting me. The cook told me that Adila was spending the evening at the bedside of a dying man at the hospital run by her family in what had formerly been the free school.

Next morning she came into my room, after first knocking at the door. She had grown a good deal thinner, and her nurse's coif made her look less ugly. But although she was barely forty she looked so old that I was appalled. My first feeling was one of horror at the idea of marrying her, because, though I was actually thirty-two, no one would have taken me for more than twenty.

Adila looked at me without saying a word. I was still lying in bed, and could see in the mirror exactly how I must appear to this aging woman whom I had got to marry. She stood there, keeping as far from me as possible, and did not even go through the motions of embracing me. She told me that she had left little Andrès in charge of a nurse at Bilbao, and that he was a very pretty baby—as though I took the slightest interest in the brat! I remember that the window was wide open. The Easter sunlight was flooding my bed, and on the leafless branches of the oaks tits were calling to one another.... There was so much young life, so much happiness, in a world which, in spite of the organized slaughter of the war, seemed full of love! I lay there looking at the woman who was to be my portion. A greying lock of hair had escaped from beneath her coif. She kept her eyes lowered, and there was a look of passive acquiescence on her face. Obviously, she had made up her mind not to look at me.

I could contain myself no longer, but broke into a babble of words:

"You've got what you wanted.... You flatter yourself that you've bought me.... You think I belong to you...but just you wait!"

She raised her eyes. I have always been able to read people's faces. There was nothing in the expression of hers that denoted greed or even violent emotion of any kind. I got out of bed, but still she looked at me. I took a few steps towards her. She was leaning against the door, and her lips were moving. She had gone so white that I asked whether I had frightened her. She nodded her head.

"Then, why are you marrying me?"

"I must. Because of Andrès."

"But you no longer love me?"

She made a vague gesture.

"You have a horror of me?"

"Not of you," she protested, "but of something in you."

"Of something in me that is evil? Well, whatever that something is, it is of your making—as you know perfectly well."

That got under her skin, and she uttered a groan.

"Don't forget, Adila, that I was a very young, a very innocent boy…a seminarian…"

Her eyes filled with tears. The poor flabby face was eloquent of fear. Suddenly she collapsed on the floor, and there was I, standing in my pajamas—you have got the scene clear, haven't you?—watching her. She had buried her head in her arms, and her heavy body was shaken by sobs. If there is one sentiment to which I am a stranger, it is pity—even for a creature to whom I may be attached by as many bonds as I was to her. Well, believe it or not, at that moment I *did* feel pity for her, pity that—how shall I put it?—was in some sense supernatural, and when I say that, I do so deliberately. In spite of myself, I protested:

"Forget it…. You're unhappy enough as it is. Forget what I said…. What's that you're muttering?"

I leaned over her and pushed aside the damp lock of hair that was plastered across her forehead. I tried to catch the words struggling through her sobs. One phrase did at last reach me:

"…a millstone were hanged about his neck…"

She repeated the threat that Christ had uttered against those who have offended against those little ones which believe in Him: "It were better for him that a millstone were hanged about his neck…"

An impulse which I found it impossible to resist brought me to my knees beside her. I took her in my arms.

"My poor dear, that threat has nothing to do with you. I was not, I never had been, one of those little ones whose angels see the Almighty face to face. As far back into my past as I can look, corruption has always been implanted in my soul. I took pleasure in troubling your peace of mind.... In such matters a man's age is of no account.... I came into the world with a gift, but it was not, as with other men, the gift of innocence, but of wearing on my face the mask that apes innocence. Between the lashes of my childish eyes, I watched the working of the temptation I had awakened in your heart and body. I felt that in me your soul had found a terrible source of danger, and the realization filled me with delight. I knew that I was the bait of the trap set to catch you. My mouth was filled with the taste of my own poison. You drew close to a body that was possessed of evil. You prowled around the false candor of my nature. Tremblingly you approached, withdrew, returned—and all the time I was on the watch. Nothing escaped me. I was a child with a heart of ice, and I played with you. Don't worry. Of the two of us, it was I who was the tempter. I was stronger and older than you. How very old I was at sixteen!—as old as the world!—and you, in spite of your seven years' seniority, had the heart of a child."

She had struggled to her feet, and now stood leaning against the wall. I can still see the puffy face, the hair escaping from beneath the white coif, can still hear the note of the woodpecker, the chirping of the tits, the song of the migrant thrushes who had settled in the ivy.... It was one of the mornings of Holy Week.... Of all the moments of my life that was the only one in which my actions were not evil. What I did then was good, for I held back a living soul from the very brink of despair.... In spite of myself, no doubt, in spite of myself, but in spite of someone else too.

"You must run away...from me!" I said it not once, but again and again. "Take advantage of this moment. Make your escape!"

She shook her head, and the eyes with which she fixed me held a deep tenderness. Now and again a fit of trembling caught her, but she had stopped crying. She kept on saying—"Impossible!" and at the sound of that word I recovered my normal tone of voice.

"Aren't you cured of me, then?" I asked.

She jerked upright as though I had pricked her. But I pressed my advantage:

"If you really were cured of me, you would run away as fast as your legs could carry you. Don't you realize what I have got in store for you?"

She said that she did.

"You think you know me...but you have no conception of what I am capable..." (It was as though I wanted her to become, as though she *had* to become, my wife with her eyes open.)

"How should I not have?"

There was a flatness in the voice in which she asked that question; a flatness in which I thought I could detect a note of disgust; and at that my anger blazed anew:

"We'll see whether you're so proud once the deed is done!"

With her head thrown back she pressed against the wall, and stared at me.

"I am impatient to get it finished with," she murmured. "The hardest thing of all will be to tell…"

I interrupted her roughly, but she went on:

"It's not of my mother that I am thinking. I have long prepared her mind for what is to happen. The news will not surprise her. No, I was thinking of Mathilde.…"

Why did she speak to me of Mathilde? We had always avoided, both of us, any mention of that name. I remembered that Mathilde was in England. How could she possibly concern us? We should confront her with the accomplished fact.

In a low voice Adila continued: "She is coming home tomorrow."

She stared into space, and two tears were trickling down her cheeks.

"I shall have to tell her."

"What's she got to do with it? She's only your cousin, though I suppose you've both lived in the same house, of course.… I suppose you realize that I shall take you to Paris."

I bit my lip, annoyed to think that I had given myself away, instead of waiting until we were married before announcing that I planned to leave Liogeats. But I saw that my words had left her indifferent. She was entering on marriage much as she might have thrown herself into the sea.

"Paris or elsewhere…" she murmured.

"You're right. In Paris or elsewhere you will be with me as my wife, for better or for worse, flesh of my flesh."

In a low voice she said: "I am that already."

At the sound of those words I pressed her hard:

"Given over to me bound hand and foot, Adila: my chattel, alone, isolated. There will be no one to come between us."

I had a feeling that I had failed to dominate her. She did not quail under my glance, but stood up sturdily to the attack I levelled at her.

"No, I shall not be alone: I am not alone now. If I had been I should have fled from you long ago to the end of the world, or into the world beyond."

I could think of no answer, and after a moment's silence, she went on:

"I shall speak to my mother…but Mathilde is more than I can manage. You must tell her the news yourself…and the sooner the better…tomorrow. We must get it all finished quickly…why not in Paris, since that is where you are legally domiciled?"

"No," I protested: "I want a church marriage, here. I want you to walk through Liogeats in your white dress. I want our neighbors to be present at my triumph…a fine triumph, eh? Some of them have a shrewd idea of what has happened, and you must expect a few snubs, my girl. Well, you must put up with that! I insist on a slap-up wedding in Liogeats church."

"You shall have it; we shall have it." She never took her eyes from my face, and her breathing was quick and sharp.

All that day I saw no one. I dared not venture into the village, filled as it was with war-widows and with mothers who had lost their sons. Not a house but was in mourning, not a family but lived in an agony of suspense. In those days people could not bear to see an able-bodied young man in civilian clothes. As a matter of fact, my discharge on grounds of health was perfectly genuine. The state of one of my lungs, as revealed by auscultation and the X-ray, still gave cause for a good deal of anxiety. The odd thing was that it did not worry me. I never felt tired. I was as strong as a horse. Explain it how you will, I was, in some odd way, being shielded—there's no getting away from it—kept in safety.... Yes, the clearer the lines of my destiny became, the more it terrified me.

I spent the day hanging about the garden. Adila had gone back to the hospital. For several years now her mother had given up coming down to meals. The old lady's windows in the main front of the chateau were the only ones to have their shutters thrown back. All the others were tight closed. I saw a servant washing down the windows of Mathilde's room, which communicated with Adila's in the west wing.

At noon I got a letter from Aline. Its tone was imperious and threatening. But it entirely failed to disturb me. It was to her interest not to put a spoke in the wheel of my marriage, and I had nothing to fear so long as the money-bags were not safely in my hands. Only when I was sure of them would she launch her attack. I trembled to think what would happen then. People of your sort, dear, reverend sir, constantly wonder how people of my sort can ever seriously think of doing away with those who stand in their path. From that moment one of my main preoccupations was to discover some way of getting rid of Aline. I had a fertile imagination and spent my whole time suppressing her—in thought. What a number of crime stories I could write with the material which my inventiveness provided me at that time! But no such thing as the perfect crime exists. Besides, Aline had long been trained in the dangerous school of blackmail, and was perpetually on her guard. She often spoke about this temptation of mine, referring to it as to something self-obvious. She would explain how it was that I should never kill her, *could* never kill her—the reason being that within forty-eight hours I should be suspected and picked up by the police. Everything would conspire to give me away. Besides—and this she told me more than once—she had confided to safe hands certain documents which would at once turn the eyes of the Law in my direction. The old bitch finally convinced me that my interest lay in her remaining alive, and that if anything happened to her, no matter how innocent I might be, I shouldn't stand a chance.

The day passed for me in the wild and leafless woods. Who I was they did not know, though they had been familiar with me since my childhood. Only men of my kind can truly love the adorable world of nature, because it is without eyes to see, without conscience to judge us. It is a world full of sweet scents, of beasts, and of stars; a world that recks nothing of saint or sinner, of those that are saved or of those that are damned. About three o'clock, I remember, I sat down on a felled pine trunk whose vast girth had stripped the oak trees in its fall. There, with the smell of torn bark about me, I enjoyed the warmth of the day as innocently as any fox or forest bird. Nature was not concerned to call me to account. All creatures living in close communion with her, and forming part of her most secret life, devour one another. I was but one among a thousand beasts of prey who at that very moment were enjoying the heat of the sun on plumage, pelt, or wing case. I was free from mental suffering. By some miracle it had withdrawn awhile. I tell you this because it is important that you should realize that, as a rule, I was never, for a single moment, without a terrible agony of mind, a frightful sense, that never left me, of being caught in a vice which would not let me go.

At that time I had not yet heard what one of your lot said to me later, an old priest with the face of a saint whom I used occasionally to meet on the winding roads of Super-Bagnères when I was taking a cure at Luchon. We were talking of the "prince of this world"—as he called him. Suddenly he said, in a tone of such certainty that it turned my blood cold: *"There are human souls that have been given to him...."* I got the impression that he knew what he was talking about. I dared not question him, and hurriedly changed the subject. Since that day I have looked everywhere for the old fellow, so as to make him explain what he meant. I did, finally, get on his tracks, but only to find that he had just died in what I believe you call "the odor of sanctity," in a home for aged priests at Vanves, taking his terrible secret with him: *"There are human souls that have been given to him...."*

MATHILDE arrived next day, after luncheon. I was not there to meet her. All afternoon I heard her calling to Adila, laughing and singing as she moved about her room, unpacking, slamming the doors. In just such a way, when she was a little girl, had everything seemed to come to life as she went through the house, and it was the same now. She had not changed. I was sitting in the sun, reading the papers, when suddenly a hand snatched off my hat. There was a burst of familiar laughter. I recognized it, but at first it was the only thing about her that I did recognize. This tall, lanky girl, with the darting movements of a swallow, had little about her to remind me of the sallow, ailing child who had been the partner of my games. Nor did she resemble the Mathilde Desbats she afterwards became, the Madame Symphorien Desbats whose spiritual director you no longer have the honor to be. Anything less tragic than the Mathilde of that time it would be hard to imagine. There was nothing about her then of that imposing presence which you knew.... Scared...yes, she certainly was that. She was like a swallow that has got into a room by mistake, and bumps against all the furniture. She was too thin, too angular.... Standing there in the middle of the garden path, like a bird that has alighted for a brief moment, she swung her hat and stared at me with little jerky movements of her small head with its thick-growing hair. I could describe to you today exactly how she was dressed, her arms bare, in spite of the weather which was still far from warm, with a great string of coral beads round her brown throat. I was no longer myself: I did not know who I was. A mysterious tide of tenderness welled up from the depths of my being and spread over the surface of my evil life. I had become once again a young boy in the presence of a young girl. My whole past existence seemed like something seen in a dream, something without reality. I was back in the days when we used to play hide-and-seek behind the privet hedge, when Adila was "he," trying to find us, calling our names, while I crouched with my arms about her, not holding her tight, and hers were round my neck. All the squalor of my life was no more than the substance of a quick nightmare from which I had waked with a start to find her still there, still my little sweetheart, both of us waiting for something to happen, both of us careful not to precipitate a decision.

Suddenly she spoke: "You're not a bit different, dear little Gabriel: you still blush as you always did...."

Fatal words! At once the mist cleared, and I saw my life as it was.

Had it, then, left no mark upon me? But, indeed, what Mathilde had just said was almost true. In the days when we used to play together, I had been as much a lost soul as I am now—only the seeming innocence of childhood had concealed the truth.... No, I had not changed. Whatever my subsequent actions, I had added nothing to my true features, to my features as they were laid up in eternity.

"You don't *look* ill...though you must be. Oh, I know all about it. When I was here last I had a squint at your X-ray pictures.... I'm no end of a dab at medicine, you know! It really is quite extraordinary how healthy you look."

She asked about my temperature, and seemed to be quite put out to hear that I did not take it every evening. We wandered off together. A great number of pines had been felled, and the clearings thus made had destroyed our remembered haunts. Once, in order to reach the banks of the Balion, which in those days had flowed through a tangled shade of oaks and alders, we had had to force a path through a mass of underbrush. Now its surface was naked to the sky, and it rippled through a great expanse of bare ground dotted with tree stumps and covered with a scatter of bark.

"Well, anyhow the Balion itself hasn't changed," said Mathilde.

"Do you think that even bombardment, even gas could hurt a stream? There's no way in which one can injure raining water...."

"Yes, my child, there is"—(I had always called her "my child")—"one can poison it.... Hullo! Our 'jouquet's' still there!"

I take it that you know what we mean by a "jouquet" in Liogeats—a sort of a hut, a hide-out used for pigeon shooting. We entered it now, just as we used to do. It no more occurred to me to turn our isolation to account than it occurred to Mathilde to be on her guard. We had met again like two children who for many years had spent their summer holidays in the same stretch of country. In perfect simplicity we stood side by side, our shoulders touching, and once again, in that wide silence filled with the scent of dead bracken, I lost all sense of my identity. I could almost believe that the actions which had left no tell-tale mark upon my face had similarly spared my soul. Perhaps Mathilde, in her youth and freshness, had enough of innocence for the two of us? For the space of a few moments I knew happiness.... Oh yes, I *do* know what happiness can mean...until she said:

"I say, Adila *is* changed...I hardly recognized her; she looks like an old woman."

I made no reply. A few drops of rain splashed noisily on our roof of leaves and bracken. Somewhere quite close a bird was singing shrilly. I mustn't think of Adila! I mustn't think of Adila! But no matter how hard I tried to keep her at a distance, there she was, for the rest of the afternoon, between us. Mathilde asked me what I was doing with myself, and how I was managing to live. My replies to her questions were very carefully worded, but I was a prey to secret dread. She was one of those thoroughly practical girls, well versed in business matters, whom one frequently meets in our part of the world, and I had the greatest difficulty in putting her off the scent. Fortunately, some of my activities were above board and could be discussed openly. At that time one could buy almost anything, hold it for a month, and then re-sell at a high profit. Mathilde pulled a face. She called that sort of thing "living from hand to mouth."

"Haven't you ever thought of leaving Paris and coming back to Liogeats for good?" she asked.

"What should I do at Liogeats?"

"How do I know? Find something."

Our eyes met in the darkness of the hut. The rain had stopped. The smell and the feel of damp earth wrapped us round…but we were warm enough. I knew what it was she was offering me. I understood…but, alas, it was too late! Unless I was prepared to sacrifice Adila…not that she *would* be sacrificed. Adila no longer loved me. She looked on our marriage as nothing more than an act of reparation. She had no weapon against me.

"You might, for instance, look after my property—why not?"

"In what capacity?"

She avoided the question, began to talk in a desultory way about Brighton, and told me of two friends of hers, Australian girls, whose parents had gone down on a torpedoed ship. Suddenly she asked whether I knew why she had come back to France. There was a plan afoot for her to marry one of her cousins—Symphorien Desbats—a man twenty years her senior, who had been looking after her land even while her parents were alive. I showed vague signs of emotion.

"I've not made up my mind yet what answer to give," she said, "but if, as seems probable, it's going to be *No*, I can hardly refuse by letter a man to whom I owe so much…."

It had begun to rain again. We ran all the way back to the house. I had taken her hand as I always had done when we were children, but now she was quicker on her feet than I was. Thus, hand in hand, we entered the dark hall. The storm was rumbling faintly in the distance. I noticed a nurse's cape lying on one of the chairs.

"Adila's back," said Mathilde. "I don't quite like to call her, because I've got a feeling that she's avoiding me. Can you think of any reason why she should be angry with me? Perhaps she thinks I didn't write to her often enough…but, after all, we've never been on very intimate terms. Oh well, when I'm married I shall have a home of my own at last."

"Isn't the chateau owned jointly by you two?"

"I shall get out…it doesn't mean a thing to me.… If Adila wants to keep it…"

"Monsieur Desbat's house on the Square is a gloomy sort of place."

In a voice that trembled she said there was no question of her living "in Monsieur Desbat's house."

As usual, whenever there was a storm, the electric lights had been switched off. We were still standing, and all round us was the rustle of rain in the dusk. We heard steps on the first floor. I was seized by a mad unreasoning desire to tell Adila everything at once, to throw her overboard. I just couldn't wait a moment longer in a condition of uncertainty. All I wanted was that the way should be made clear for me, so that I might at last have a chance of being happy. I would sweep all obstacles aside. In imagination I was already rushing to do them battle, like a man possessed. And what about Aline? Well, Mathilde was as rich as Adila…and I could divert a sum large enough to keep Aline's mouth shut.... But that, of course, was nonsense. I knew only too well that nothing would stop the wretched creature from levying blackmail on me until I had got her out of the way for good and all. Once the marriage was an accomplished fact I should have to begin thinking seriously about that. The mere fact of happiness, of a happiness such as I had never dreamed of having, would give me courage to reduce Aline to silence—to the silence of eternity. Yes, on the spur of the moment, standing there in the entrance hall of a country house, within touching distance of a young girl whose hurried breathing I could hear beside me, I decided on that one last crime which would give me the right never to commit another. One more crime, and then, never again! The rain was making a great deal of noise. The storm was bursting over our heads, but all I could hear was the faint sound of Mathilde's rapid breathing. I stretched out my hands fumblingly in the darkness.

"Ever since we first knew one another!" she murmured. "And you?"

I held her in my arms, but could not keep my mind from the noise of those heavy footsteps above our heads. Adila...I must get rid of Adila at once...I could not remain in suspense a moment longer. Very gently I pushed Mathilde aside, telling her to go to her room and wait for me there.

I burst in on Adila without knocking, like a thief. She was pacing up and down saying her rosary. It was the sound of that continual pacing that we had heard downstairs in the hall.

Candles were burning on the mantelpiece. My appearance seemed to disturb her, and she stopped, her rosary wound about her wrist.

"I wanted to have a word with you before dinner"—how gentle my voice was; its gentleness surprised even me—"I've been thinking over what we were saying yesterday. I've done you enough harm already, my poor Adila.... It would be madness for us to get married...."

Her gesture was eloquent of weariness. "What use is there in going over all that again? Everything that could be said has been said already."

I stumbled over my words. I was in the grip of a blind rage.

"And what about me? What's going to happen to me? How about *my* happiness?"

Adila turned and looked at me intently: "Your *happiness*? It's my fortune, my property."

She spoke with an air of complete detachment. I protested that I didn't give a fig for her property. I tried in vain to control myself. "I can have just as good—a better property than yours...and marry a woman into the bargain who won't be..." (Here I uttered one of those words that occasionally slip from me...one of those gutter words that are not really typical of me at all, because, ordinarily, I recoil from using them. But you wouldn't believe the kind of language that rises to my lips on occasion....)

In a trembling voice Adila put a question: "What woman? Mathilde? I thought as much...I felt it coming." The last words she added with a look of deep distress. Then, very calmly:

"Oh no, my dear, you had better give up all thought of any such thing."

"Who's going to stop me?" I blustered.

She replied that she had ways and means.

"It would be the end of you."

I was in one of those paroxysms of rage from the effects of which she suffered more than once. But she did not so much as flinch, but kept her eyes steadily fixed on me.

"You're not frightening me. I'm prepared for anything. Listen carefully. I will gladly incriminate myself if, by that means, I can save Mathilde. Don't you yet realize that I have nothing more to lose, nothing more to gain, that I have already lost all or gained all…that you no longer have it in your power to do me either good or harm?"

I raised my hands to the level of her fat white neck:

"Doesn't that frighten you?"

She shook her head:

"No, because you are much too frightened yourself, Gabriel."

I almost leapt at her as she left the room. She went as far as the landing, but not, as I had at first thought, with the idea of escaping from me, for I heard her call Mathilde's name in a firm voice.

The stairs creaked under the younger girl's light tread. I was standing as far as possible from the window, and Mathilde did not at first see me when she came into the room. I heard her speak:

"Are you there, Gabriel?"

Adila closed the door.

"Gabriel and I cannot wait any longer to tell you the great news. You promised me that you would tell Mathilde yourself…."

The girl must have at first believed that I had just been

speaking of what had occurred between us, and that Adila had countered by announcing her own engagement.

"So we've both of us found happiness," she said with a smile. "Who is he, Adila? Do tell me. Do I know him?"

"Can't you guess, darling? He is here in the room with us."

She was feeling her way. I heard Mathilde reply—I felt as though I was dreaming.

"But…you must be joking!"

I was waiting for the final blow to fall, when, suddenly, the girl flung a question at me:

"This isn't true, Gabriel, is it?"

I brought out my answer with difficulty:

"I sincerely hope not.…"

In a completely colorless voice, as though she were repeating a lesson, Adila assured her cousin that we were engaged, and that I could not deny it. Mathilde's voice hissed rather than spoke:

"Is she laughing at you? Answer! Say something!"

I made a vague gesture of denial. I heard Mathilde's breathless words without attaching any significance to them.

My mind remained a blank for what seemed an age. Then understanding returned. I could grasp what she was saying in a voice that trembled with emotion:

"It's as clear to me as daylight. It never occurred to you that I should be such a fool…but you knew that *she'd* consent. The only thing *you* cared about was worming your way into the family in any way you could. I should never have believed you capable of such cold-blooded calculation, Gabriel!"

The memory of Adila's expression will remain with me forever.

"Who would have thought it!" said her cousin. Certainly, to anyone who knew the facts of my life, Mathilde's incredulity must have seemed highly comic.

"Don't worry! *I* shan't try to get him away from you. It would be easy enough if I wanted to. But you can keep him, my dear!"

And then she said again, in a sort of semi-patois: "Keep 'im!"

Adila moved away from the wall. She had closed her eyes and said very quickly:

"It's not a question of me…but… we've got a little boy. He's called Andrès, and he's five years old.…"

Mathilde stood there as though stunned. "You? A child?" she muttered, and burst out laughing.

At last she left the room, stumbling as she went, and we heard her collapse in the corridor. I made for the door, but Adila roughly pushed me back. It would have been dangerous to resist her at that moment. I left her on her knees by the body, supporting her cousin's head, and went downstairs without once looking back.

The puddles were cold under my feet. The garden path glimmered white, but, even so, I kept on losing it and bumping against the trees. I know beyond a shadow of doubt that I have never been nearer to killing myself than then. But a muffled, fretful voice kept on repeating; "No, you're too great a coward," as though someone were speaking who was not sure of himself. It is true: I *am* a coward, and it sometimes happens that, of all our vices, cowardice is the one which proves, as often as not, to be our salvation. I went back to the house through the darkness. I was soaked to the skin, famished, and with blood on my hands; but, unfortunately, I was alive, only too much alive!

I must really hurry, my dear sir, or you'll never have the patience to follow my story to the end. Next morning, Mathilde went away, and Adila became once more the indifferent, passive, resigned creature whom I had found on my return to Liogeats. Our marriage was not, after all, celebrated in the village. I received a number of abominable letters signed by war-widows and seriously wounded men. People came and rattled tin kettles under the windows of the chateau. I had to make my escape by car, under cover of darkness, and take the train at a distant station. Adila joined me in Paris where we were married in the presence of no one but our witnesses. A few weeks later Mathilde married Symphorien Desbats.

I had insisted on a settlement by the terms of which all property should be held in common. Adila obeyed my demands without discussions. With complete disregard for Andrès' interests, she agreed to have a large number of her trees felled, to sell part of her land, and to have the money paid into my account. I drafted a will, and she signed it. Not that there was any reason to think that she would die. I don't want you to think...to suspect.... She fell a victim to influenza rather more than a year after the Armistice, just when the doctors seemed to be getting the epidemic under control. She made what you priests call "a good death," but without any fuss or bother. I did, however, hear through the door something that she said. Her thoughts were entirely of me, and she did not so much as mention her son's name. It is, you must admit, an odd sort of faith that entails redemption by suffering, and the sacrifice of a life that is not ours to give. But, then, perhaps the truth always is odd. I don't suppose you would believe me, would you, if I told you that I actually shed tears, and that I think of her as of someone who is still alive, still part of my existence?

Naturally, no sooner was I free than Aline was all for marrying me. But, as she very soon realized, I would rather have done a stretch of hard labor than make her my wife. She became quite pitiless in her levying of blackmail, and I had to go for help to Symphorien Desbats.

You know what he is like. At that time he was already a sick man. It wasn't, as they say, any excess of sentiment that made him short of breath. Had Mathilde married a man like me she would at least have known the meaning of love. True, her awakening would have been terrible, but for some weeks, perhaps even for some months, she would have known the meaning of love. You can guess the sort of married life she had. Still, she did produce a daughter, Catherine, though no sooner was the child born than she found her place already filled. When Adila died, Mathilde had written that she would like to take full responsibility for Andrès, and he has been tied to her apron-strings ever since.

Symphorien Desbats summed me up at the first glance. Not that he was capable of sounding the confused depths of my character. To imagine what a man of my sort is really like would be quite beyond his powers. He saw me as a mere product of the gutter, and, so far as the matter in hand was concerned, it was the best thing he could do. I had inherited from Adila all the money that the Law allows a testator to leave away from a son in the interests of a husband. The demands made upon me by Aline—and also, I must confess, the kind of life I was leading (what a life!)—compelled me, before long, to fell what remained of my pines, first the older trees, then those in full yield. One day, in Paris, Symphorien Desbats came to see me. He told me that I was ruining the property, and that I had better hand over the management of it to him. He would guarantee me an adequate income. He began by advancing all the money I asked for. I will spare you the story of the various tricks he played in order to get me to sell him my woods which, of course, marched with his. As Andrès grew up, he had recourse to a line of action which, no doubt, justified me in my own eyes—as though a man like me needs justification!—but I do, where my son's future is in question, but which, more important still, left Mathilde, his wife, without the power to resist. For Mathilde championed Andrès against me as though he had been her own child. You know her. Well enough by this time to realize how much fonder she is of him than of Catherine. I remember how furious she was with her husband when she realized that he was making use of my perpetual need of money in order to strip me bare....

But Desbats countered her indignation by arguing that, since there was no way of keeping me from selling my land to the first bidder, it was very much better to prevent it from going out of the family. The only way of ensuring that Andrès' future should not be jeopardized was to arrange for him and Catherine to be engaged, so that he might be certain of recovering by marriage what his father had surrendered for ready cash. There was nothing intrinsically absurd about the scheme, because, from their earliest years, Andrès and Catherine had been inseparable. There seemed to be no good reason for thinking that Symphorien was not acting in perfect good faith. He had that love of land which leads men to dread above all things the breaking up of estates among a number of heirs, and is the reason why, in France, we see so many marriages between blood-relations. What it all came to was this: that he was forking out money to keep my land in the family. Sooner or later, Andrès would get control of the property.

In this way Desbats made sure of his wife's neutrality in a campaign which had as its object the buying up by degrees of everything that stood in my name. Andrès' ownership of the two tenant farms of Cernes and Balizaou remained undisturbed. He had inherited them from his mother, and they were entirely outside my power to control. They amounted, in round figures, to about 2,500 acres. But why, if Desbats is really planning to marry our two children, is he going to all this trouble in order to get his hands on what remains of the boy's patrimony? Why should he saddle himself with legal charges so as to get possession of what, in the ordinary course of events, will be my son's marriage portion? That is what I can't understand, and, believe me, it gives me a considerable headache! I know that since he has become half paralyzed, his passion for land has taken on the form of a regular mania. It's impossible to argue with him…. He goes so far as to say that the clinching of the bargain is a necessary preliminary to the match. He is bringing every kind of pressure on me to persuade Andrès to sell. I don't know whether you realize it, but, odd sort of father that I am—and by this time you should have a pretty clear idea of what I'm like—I do completely dominate that boy of mine, though I've never taken the slightest interest in him since the day he was born, and he never sees me except when I come back to Liogeats with the sole object of replenishing my pockets with money which, in fact, I have stolen from him. My power to exercise charm has certainly not stopped short of my son! He is my latest conquest, and I am busy exploiting him as I have always exploited others—with this difference, that I happen to be very fond of him.

He will do everything I ask him, though he, too, has the land in his blood. But, in his case, the passion is neither mean nor grasping. He lacks the instinct of possession. But, as though to make up for its absence, he has inherited from his mother a keen interest in the welfare of his tenants. He keeps a watchful eye on all that concerns them...he's "on their side"—to quote a malicious saying of his employer—and *employer* is the right word, seeing that what he has really become is the public-spirited bailiff of Symphorien Desbats. Not satisfied with owning most of the Du Buch property, this old fox is now treating the last male descendant of the line as a species of domestic servant. And Andrès puts up with it all because he thinks himself as good as married to Catherine. He is prepared to fall in with what he regards as a sick man's whim, and will part with Balizaou and Cernes at a rock-bottom price in order to cut the legal dues to the lowest possible figure. He is even more ready to do this because Desbats has taken a solemn oath that he will fix the date of the wedding as soon as the business has finally been put through. But I want him to hang on to the farms. I am perfectly well aware that, if the deal goes through, I stand to pocket a commission—the purchase-price was arranged between Desbats and me—and the boy, who knows how hard-pressed I am, has promised to let me have the proceeds of the sale on loan at 5 percent. But how can I be sure that the whole thing isn't a trap, that the old man won't refuse to have the boy as his son-in-law once he's fleeced him? How can one trust the word of a man like that unless it's been duly sworn in front of a lawyer? The real trouble is that Aline is becoming more and more exorbitant in her demands. In days gone by I had several strings to my bow…but I am getting older with every month and every week that passes.…

Well, things can't be much worse for me than they are already, and I am not going to be a party to seeing the boy robbed.… He's got to hang on to Cernes and Balizaou…at least until the marriage is an accomplished fact. Besides, present loss is future gain. Once I'd touched my commission and got that loan out of Andrès, there'd be nothing for me to fall back on. Perhaps I'd better throw myself on Desbats' mercy… for he may be able to settle Aline for me, unless, of course, he makes use of what I've told him in confidence to cook my goose for good and all, and makes it an excuse for calling the marriage off.… Only you, Monsieur l'Abbé, only you.…

1.

THE man laid down his fountain-pen, read through what he had written, and got up. He was wearing a dressing gown of blue silk, much torn and stained. His dark, tanned face looked young in spite of his silvery hair. Probably his light-colored, sharp eyes had not changed much since his boyhood. A melancholy daylight filtered through the dirty windows, that Paris daylight which one waits impatiently to see fade before closing the flimsy iron shutters which have a way of nipping one's fingers. The furniture dated from 1925. The passing years had not improved the distempered wall or the objects of glass and nickel that stood about the room. Nothing would change their look of raw newness until the next upheaval of the world. Nevertheless, the general impression made by the place was one of untidiness, not the untidiness that makes a house look lived-in, but, rather, the sort of abandonment that broods over ruins. A tray with the remains of a cold meal had been dumped on the floor. Cigarette ends lay about everywhere. It was obvious that no one had done any cleaning for several days.

Gabriel Gradère lay down on the divan which served him as a bed. "What point is there in writing all this?" he said to himself. "What can that wretched priest do to help…? Besides, *I won't* see him, *I won't* make his acquaintance, *I won't* let him come meddling in my secrets!"

A child on the floor above began to practice scales. Gradère was conscious of a feeling of relief, for he hated silence. It was as though silence had a life of its own, as though it breathed. The atmosphere of the room was heavy, stuffy, and used-up. He felt he could not stay there a moment longer…. Hurriedly he took off his dressing gown and put on his clothes. What a relief to slam the door behind him, to turn the key in the lock as though he were imprisoning within the walls of this room in the Rue Emile-Zola the mortal enemy of his life and of life in general.

It was the time of day when all the street-lamps go on at once. He walked quickly. His movements were those of a young man, and very characteristic. It was as though he had wings on his heels. He bought a paper. He felt like a man who is throwing somebody off his tracks. Who, seeing him there, could have put a name to him? He crossed the Seine and followed the tram lines as far as the Porte d'Auteuil. He passed a café. In summer the tables outside would have been thronged with people, but there was no one there now. He did not feel the cold; he never did. A Pernod…. One can never be quite sure that it will produce the hoped-for state of mental bliss…. Sometimes it opens a way of escape…but alcohol is equally capable of adding to one's sense of misery, of putting a fine edge on despair…. But this particular Pernod would brim with mercy, would make it possible for him to go home with all his fears allayed, to lie down and close his eyes. He would save money by having no dinner. He would go out later, sit at the table where the same woman was to be found each evening at the *Florence,* and would order a sandwich for which she would pay, plus a bottle of champagne. Nevertheless, he shivered slightly in the damp night air. A breath of the country, smelling of leaves and mold, drifted over the Quarter. He hurried home.

"Heavens!" he said to himself: "I quite forgot to switch off the lights! Aline! What on earth are you doing here? You know I told you not to come and see me...."

The woman, who lay crumpled up on the divan, made no movement. She was smoking. An empty bottle of port stood beside her. She had perched her hat on the head of a Buddha standing on the mantelpiece. Her large face looked as though it had been plastered all over with flour. It was thickly painted but had not been washed. Two fuddled, watery eyes peered out at him from super-imposed layers of make-up. A line of purplish lip stick marked the position of the slit which did service for a mouth. Her skirt, pulled above her knees, revealed a pair of still handsome legs in imitation silk stockings.

"I don't care what you told me. I've got a key, haven't I? I'm sick of waiting: I've been doing nothing else for two months."

She had kept her Bordeaux accent. Gabriel sat down beside her, lit a cigarette, and, in winning, humble tones said:

"But there's nothing I can do, Aline...I have to be content with one meal a day...."

"You can touch the kid, can't you?"

He interrupted her roughly:

"You leave the kid out of it! I'm not going to rob Andrès. That's something I won't do. I've said no to that once, and I say it again!"

"But he's perfectly willing…"

"All the more reason for not abusing his goodness of heart.…"

"But his marriage depends on the deal. You've got Desbats' promise, and he's never gone back on his word yet.…"

Gabriel shook his head but made no reply.

"Find some other way, then.… Doesn't matter to me if the kid's done down.… You'll have to come to it sooner or later, you old twister. You know perfectly well there's nothing else you *can* do. But meanwhile…"

She dwelt on the ends of her words in a kind of singsong. He was standing by the radiator, looking at her—forcing himself to look at her. He must finish once and for all with this woman…chuck her out. Why not tonight? She couldn't make her threats good…it would be too dangerous. The last thing in the world she wanted was to attract the attention of the police.

"I know what you're thinking," she said suddenly. He gave a start. She asked him for a cigarette and stretched out a hand with spatulate fingers. The red nails had the effect of accentuating its grubbiness.

"You're telling yourself I shan't do anything. Well, my lad, you're wrong.… There's a lot you don't know."

Aline had made him sit down beside her, so that she could speak with the advantage of close proximity.

"Suppose that someone you've treated pretty badly… someone whose life you've smashed, as the saying goes…

someone you've dishonored…someone pretty high up who doesn't care what he spends…has sworn to get even with you, no matter how much it costs."

"I don't know who you're talking about," he stammered. But, at once, several names came to his mind. "In any case," he went on in a more determined voice, "if the gentleman in question is going to get even with me, I shan't take the knock by myself, that I swear.… It's no use your trying to put it over me like that.…"

"Silly boy! What d'you take me for?"

She chuckled, keeping her mouth closed so as not to show her teeth.

"The day he starts getting busy it'll be time for me to pack up. The gentleman in question, as you call him, has accepted all my conditions. He's prepared to maintain me abroad…in some nice, quiet little place.… Don't you believe me?"

"No, because if what you're saying were true, you'd have swallowed the bait already…I don't suppose it's out of any love for me that…"

"It certainly isn't, my pet! The truth is, I've got settled into my little ways here. Travelling doesn't tempt me. Paris is the only place one can live really well in…I'm not trying to put it over you. It's all to my interest that you and I should reach a friendly agreement, but you've got to play *your* part…you've got to do the right thing by me."

She spoke calmly, without any show of anger. This sort of bargaining was second nature to her.

He put a question, but did not sound at all sure of himself.

"This fellow you're talking about—I suppose it's the Marquis, eh?"

"No good trying to hide anything from you! Just do a bit of thinking for a change…those letters of his wife's…the amount you made him cough up…. But it's not just a question of the dough…you know what that woman meant to him…. The woman you stole and dragged through every kind of dirt… and then his daughter's marriage which was broken off as a result…. The girl's become a nervous wreck…. Crazy would be nearer the mark, I should say…she's had to be shut up."

"It was you made me do it. Besides," he added quickly, "if it hadn't been me it would have been someone else…. What's the use of going over all that again?"

"*I'm* not going over anything. It was you who started in on this…. Well, what about it?"

This time he answered in an entirely different tone of voice:

"I'm off to Liogeats tomorrow…you'd better clear out now. But don't run away with the idea that I believe you. The Marquis de Dorth has a horror of scandal…knows too much about it…. He'd pay through the nose rather than have anything to do with a woman of your sort…."

She was not in the least put out:

"You don't really think, do you, that he honors me with his presence? Everything's done on the q. t. through a third party. He means to get even with you all right, but it'll be managed very quietly, without any fuss or bother…."

He pushed her, resisting, towards the door.

"Why not send a telegram? I've got to have some money at once…."

"No, something's still to be fixed up about the commission. But the important thing is that I must have a definite assurance that Andrès' marriage is going through before I take any definite steps...."

She wrapped herself in an old, moth-eaten fur cloak.

"I'll give you a week.... If, next Monday, at this time... I'm quite a decent sort, now aren't I?"

As soon as he was alone, Gabriel opened the window and breathed in the damp air. He swung round sharply. He could have sworn that somebody had called his name from the corner of the room. But there was no one there. Aline's warmth was still heavy on the air. The place was full of her smell, saturated with the stench of her gross body. He shut the window, and said, out loud:

"There's no one here."

His roving eyes took in the walls, the ceiling, the carpet. Suddenly, in a mood of feverish haste, he snatched up his hat, his overcoat.... Once again he set out aimlessly along the Quays—deserted at this hour. Though he was oppressed by an immense weariness, his stride was rapid, youthful, almost winged.

2.

◆

THE local train, after prolonged whistling, got itself into motion and ran on until it came to a stop in Liogeats station. It was ten o'clock at night. Gabriel, a felt hat pulled low over his face, gave up his ticket to the porter, and then, instead of crossing the booking hall which was filled with people who had come to buy their evening papers, took a path that led round behind the station. Threading his way between stacks of planks standing in the yard of the saw mill, he reached the moonlit road.

The bag which he was carrying in his right hand was not heavy. This particular road was known locally as the "Boulevard" because it circled the little town which, at this hour, was already asleep. To his left the pines pressed in upon it. The milky darkness, dripping through their high crests, ran down the scaly trunks and flowed over the rough tangle of brushwood at their feet. To his right lay the town, hidden now by the mist rising from the river bed and the low-lying pastures. It seemed more silent than the forest whence came the occasional cry of some night-prowling animal, and, at intervals, the sound of a falling cone. But the townspeople, worn out after the day's work, were fast asleep in their lairs. The merged breathing of the exhausted human herd was inaudible.

The road crossed the Balion. Gabriel could hear its water flowing over the pebbly bed with the unbroken murmur to which he had listened as a child. All around him stretched that world of material things which, though they pass no judgment on our actions, still work upon us, wakening regrets and longings, no matter what those actions may have been. How deep, how sweet were the unconscious influences of the night!

He was walking, now, more slowly. So long as he kept to the road that lay before him white in the moon, his shadow, broken by recurrent piles of flints, roused no more sense of loathing in the earth than if it had belonged to the young priest whom, on the mad impulse of a moment, he had wished to take into his confidence. He could see the house in which the Abbé lived, gleaming, white as a leper, at a turn of the road, of that same Liogeats road where once he had run and scampered in the carefree gaiety of childhood, that road which did not know what it was that had brought him back to this country scene.... Was he himself sure what his reasons for coming had been? Had not every step in his progress been determined by obscure promptings? Ostensibly he was there to attend the sale of Cernes and Balisaou. But had not this journey of his, undertaken on the spur of the moment, been dictated by quite other motives? What secret and irreparable deed was he about to do in this remote corner of the world, where, on just such a night, he had been born, in a mean room, fifty years before?

The lessons of experience left him no excuse for self-deception. Such sudden and unpremeditated flittings had always, for him, marked the launching or completion of some scheme. He had a vague feeling that he was poised for action, that he was like a stone held in a clenched fist, inert as the pebble which, the next moment, a child will fling at some harmless beast. Never before had he been so acutely aware of this terrible state of passivity.

In spite of the mist rising from the Balion, he leaned over the parapet, and looked down at the diaphanous wisps of vapor, hearing the murmur of the stream. The water had a smell all its own that came neither from sewage nor drowned grasses, a barely perceptible scent which he had noticed even in the days of his childhood—his smirched and far from innocent childhood. Yet now the night set moving within him freshets of goodness and of love that nothing had impaired.... A sudden yearning came on him to make some gesture, perform some action, which should be at odds with his manifest destiny. But what good deed was possible on this empty road and in this sleeping world? There was no traveler lying in the ditch whom he might tend and succor, not so much as a numbed and frozen bird for him to revive.

Nevertheless, the feeling was there, the stirring of one of those impotent good intentions with which Hell is said to be paved. The ebb and flow of the whole wide world moved within him—the milky darkness, redolent of damp and chastity, the unseeing stream running between its banks and holding no memory of his childish feet in the days when he had caught crayfish with the Du Buch girls.... Lucky for him that these mist-drenched fields could remember nothing!

It was growing colder now, and he resumed his walk. At a turn in the road, just where the Boulevard meets the lane leading to the chateau, he saw before him the leprous ghastliness of the priest's house. Within those walls the young man lay asleep to whom he had wanted to tell the story of his life. What madness! He, too, must be stretched upon his bed, stripped of his black robe, worn out with physical fatigue and misery of heart, no different from the parishioners who tormented him, made one with them by the same exhaustion, covered by the same pall of night that lay above them all. This graveyard of the living was but a foretaste of that other graveyard where all would meet, tormentors and victims alike, on the edge of the little town....

Was the priest's sister there too, in spite of calumnies and persecution? Gabriel looked up. The moon was shining full upon the closed shutters which showed as blotches of green against the peeling walls.

What was that lying on the steps in front of the door? He gazed with curiosity at the scatter of freshly cut boughs, with, here and there, the sheen of laurel leaves. It was a local custom thus to adorn the threshold of newly wed lovers on their marriage-night.... Suddenly he realized the significance of the cruel, malicious joke. The parish was playing an ugly trick on its priest. Next morning when he left the house on his way to early Mass, this carpet of brushwood would tell him what the people of Liogeats thought of him and of the bit of skirt whom he was passing off as his sister! The day starts early at Liogeats. Even though the priest said Mass at half-past six, there would be watching eyes at shuttered windows, nasty little urchins behind the poplars on the road.

At present the tormentors were asleep. Only the moon at its zenith gazed down on the unhappy earth—and on nothing more unhappy than these boughs and laurel branches lying on the doorstep of a country priest.

Gabriel had an inspiration. He put down his bag among the nettles that grew at the foot of the low wall which separated the road from the priest's garden at the back of the house. He looked about him and listened. Not a dog was barking. He could hear only the occasional crowing of a cock cheated by the moon. He took up great armfuls of the scattered boughs and threw them over the low wall. In spite of the damp chill of the night air, he grew warm as he worked. When little remained to be done, he picked up the few remaining branches, one by one, until all had been removed. Then, slightly out of breath, he leaned for a moment against a poplar opposite the house before going on his way. The threshold, cleared of all encumbrance, looked naked under the moon. The middle of the stone steps had been worn into a depression by the feet of all those, the living and the dead, who had come this way to knock upon the door. In the moonlit darkness the old stones seemed more expressive than a human face. They quivered with a sort of muted life. The man whose impure hands had swept them bare felt suddenly as though they were looking at him. The impression lasted only for a moment. Then he took his bag, and turned sharply to his left into the avenue leading to the chateau.

3.

THE ground mist hid the fields. Beyond the lake of low-lying fog the great pines of Frontenac, set on a high mound, may have remembered what they had seen and heard. Bergère barked, and Gabriel called, "Tuchau, Bergère!"

Already in imagination he could feel the bitch's paws against his chest, her tongue warm on his neck and chin.

There was a sound of shutters being thrown back.

"Qu'ès aco?"

"It's me, Gercinthe: me, Monsieur Gabriel…."

The old woman cried down that she would be with him in a moment. He waited, sitting on his suitcase. A key turned in the lock of the kitchen door.

"So it is you?"

The deaf old creature looked at him with a suspicious eye. She alone of all the domestic staff slept at the chateau. The two young maids, daughters of one of the tenant farmers, and a manservant, lived at the farm and had their evening meal there.

The light dazzled Gabriel. He explained that, as usual, the train had been an hour late, that he had had no dinner and was as hungry as a hunter. Already Gercinthe was throwing pine-cones and shavings on the embers, and beginning to fuss. What did he want to eat? "There's not much left." She detested Gradère, but it was part of her religion to see that her masters were properly fed.

"Anything you've got!" said Gabriel.

She brought the remains of a paté de foie gras and some cold chicken—"only the carcass, but it might be worse.…"

He ate slowly, feeling a deep sense of security and well-being. Paris was far away, and Aline, and the hideous life he had been leading.… There was no one now to prod at him.

"Everyone well?"

Gercinthe embarked on a tale of woe. Monsieur Desbats had had one of his attacks…was down again with that asthma of his.… No one but his daughter could do anything for him.… Proper devoted, that was what Miss Catherine was…and him just a mass of nerves.

"A terrible thing that there asthma…but the sight of you'll quiet him down! They've been waiting for you so's they can get on with the marriage." Then, in a low voice, as though speaking to herself as she fussed round the table, she added: "Tricky as a bagful of monkeys he be!"

Gabriel stopped eating and gave her a shrewd look.

"What are you hinting at—that he doesn't want Catherine to marry the boy?"

She fell to muttering:

"Don't 'ee go putting words into my mouth. *I* didn't say nowt o' that!"

"And how's Andrès?"

"Always on the move. This week he's been a-counting of

the pines over to Jouanhaut, them as Monsieur Desbats has sold to Mouleyre.... Here be Madam...."

The woman who had just come into the room, her full figure wrapped in a purple dressing gown, was indeed Mathilde. Her thick hair, hurriedly piled on top of her head, left visible a high, lusterless forehead, and gave her an old fashioned appearance. Her rather hollow cheeks were of an unhealthy yellow, but her neck and the swell of her breast, visible beneath the loosely fastened gown, had the whiteness of a flower petal. Gabriel had risen. He alone in all the world could see in this mature, this almost heavy, woman the slim, birdlike girl whom he had loved.

It was Mathilde, and that, for him, meant always Mademoiselle Du Buch. In her presence he became once more just "young Gradère," the peasant lad from the Péloueyres, the boy whom Adila and Mathilde had always addressed in the second person singular, while he never departed from a respectful "mademoiselle."

"Sure you're not still hungry? We ought to have a serious talk, now, this evening, if you're not too sleepy. Go to bed, Gercinthe. The clearing up can wait until tomorrow morning. Don't worry about anything. I'll put the fire-guard on. Hurry up, now!" She spoke firmly and calmly, like one who is accustomed to being obeyed.

"Draw up to the fire, the nights are getting cold."

It caused her no emotion to find herself, thus circumstanced, in the great kitchen at Liogeats where, as children, they had watched preserves simmering in the copper saucepans, and across which they had scampered to crouch in the concealment of the scullery while Adila looked for them in

the garden, and cried out—"Mind, no hiding in the house!"
At such moments he had always pressed her hand, and they
had stayed where they were, speechless from sheer happiness.

Of these things she had retained no memory. The look
she fixed on him was at once preoccupied and indifferent.
He did not inspire in her even feelings of disgust. He would
rather have seen her tremble at the recollection of that day
when Adila had told her of their engagement. But nothing
was more foreign to Mathilde's nature than to chew over and
ruminate, as he did to excess, the events of the past.... What
secrets had Adila confided to her as she lay dying? Whatever
they may have been, they were now, if not forgotten, at least
buried deep in her mind. It was as though that part of her life
had been wiped away, finished, killed. All that counted with
this woman were the concerns, the people, of the present.

"You did well to come...but there must be no false move!
Symphorien is talking more than ever about going through
with the marriage. It seems to me as though it were all a little
too easy. He is *too* cheerful: there is something almost suspect
in his buoyancy."

"He is a very sick man."

"Yes, I know, but sometimes I wonder. I was reading the
other day in the *Petit Parisien* of a man who made believe that
he was very ill.... There are times when Symphorien is deaf,
so deaf that one has to shout at him, and then, quite suddenly,
he will hear something said in quite a low voice. He is paralyzed all down one side and can scarcely walk...but at times
he runs about the house as nimbly as a rat! All we know for
certain is that he is asthmatic and has overtaxed his heart. Of
course, Dr. Clairac.... Shall I tell you what I think? I think

he's got some sort of a hold over Dr. Clairac. There was rather an ugly story about an accident to one of the farmhands, and Symphorien helped to clear him. I've got an idea that he tells Dr. Clairac what he wants his diagnosis to be.... On the other hand, I don't very well see how he *can* stop Andrès' marriage now that things have gone so far. But he's such a maniac where land is concerned that he'd do everything in his power to hang on, during his lifetime, to what he calls the "two last provinces" which have not, as yet, been absorbed into the estate, those two 'fairest jewels in his crown,' Cernes and Balisaou. It's become a perfect obsession with him."

Gabriel stifled a yawn.

"Then he'd better make up his mind...."

"Yes, but the first thing we've got to do is to insist on the marriage contract being signed the same day as..."

She stared into the fire, rubbing her knees, the while, with a sort of mechanical movement. Gabriel was becoming sleepy. He could feel Bergère's warm nose against his hand. The ticking of the clock was barely audible. How far away Paris seemed, and Aline! He could hear in the chimney the sound of the wind among the pines, a prolonged moaning that neither rose nor fell, and seemed at last to make one with the silence.

"Listen to me, Gabriel."

He gave a start. Mathilde had transferred her gaze to his face. She sat there with her handsome, but rather too large hands clasped on her lap. The wide sleeves of her dressing gown revealed a pair of firm and powerful arms.

"Swear to me that he has not promised you any commission. He's a miser over money, and if he has offered you a large sum on condition that the deal goes through, that means we've been done...."

Gabriel assured her in honeyed tones that Desbats had made him no such promise.

"Is that really the truth? You're not lying to me?"

He felt the implied insult and seemed about to turn restive; but Mathilde merely shrugged her shoulders:

"It's a waste of time to try that sort of thing on with me."

"You despise me, don't you?" he asked in a low voice.

"Despise is a big word," she replied in a voice of mockery, "a word for Paris folk. Down here we don't bother our heads about loving, or despising, or all the other things you and your friends think about. The land, the poultry, the pigs are what we worry over...every thing else can go hang!"

All of a sudden he found that she was getting on his nerves, irritating him, though he did not quite know why he said:

"If you had nothing else than that to give you an interest in life..."

"What else should I have?"

"Andrès, for instance...."

She showed a vague smile.

"Naturally...he is much more my son than he is yours or Adila's.... After all, you gave him to me, didn't you? Yes, I certainly have him."

She had risen, but sat down again to talk about Andrès. Her face was radiant with happiness. The immense whispering of the pines did not break the silence. But the old sweet-smelling kitchen no longer brought to Gabriel a sense of security. He had lost the feeling of being hidden away from the dangers of life. It was as though somebody had suddenly come into the room, though the door was shut; somebody who had lost track of him since he had left Paris, but had followed post-haste and had at last succeeded in coming up with him. Perhaps it was "he" again. Was it? Bergère was fast asleep, her muzzle between her paws. Hams were hanging from the beams. On the shelves of the dresser, adorned with scalloped paper, there was a glint of copper pans and kettles. No, the kitchen had ceased to be an island of the past to which he could flee for refuge. All the horrors of his daily existence had suddenly burst in upon their silence. Had a footstep sounded in the garden, had a hand pushed open the door, it would not have surprised him to see Aline there before him, clutching her old fur coat about her shapeless body. In a flash everything had changed. But Mathilde seemed not to notice any difference. She sat there playing absent-mindedly with her wedding ring, her arm bare to the elbow.

"Are you really sure, my dear, that you are working for Andrès' happiness?"

She looked at him with surprise:

"Of course. Why do you ask?"

"Because it doesn't seem to occur to you to wonder whether Andrès will be happy with Catherine. I don't want to hurt your feelings, but this daughter of yours…"

"Oh," she exclaimed with a smile, "my feelings aren't hurt, not the least little bit in the world. Catherine is ugly, it's no good pretending she isn't—but she's no fool. Reserved, sulky, and not in the least brilliant, perhaps, but what of it? All that's true enough, but it doesn't alter the fact that she may be just the wife he needs. It has been understood ever since they were children. The land is what Andrès cares about more than anything else. The estate is his whole life—after his football. Down here, you know, men don't expect their wives to be marvels of intelligence and beauty. So long as they know how to bring up their children, so long as they are neat and clean… though in those ways I don't deny that Catherine has still got a deal to learn. I'm afraid, too, that she has no fondness for animals, and doesn't take much interest in the poultry…. But all that will come later. Besides, I shall be there."

"Yes, you will be there."

"Of course I shall. What's in your mind? Come, out with it," she said drily. "Are you afraid I may disturb the happiness of the young couple? Do you think they'll want to live in a perpetual intimacy of two? You can make your mind easy on that score. They have known one another all their lives, and there's not likely to be much romance between them. People here don't carry on like turtledoves—that's not our country way. Nothing will be changed."

"Except that they'll be sleeping in the same room."

"Naturally."

"And in the same bed."

"All right, then—in the same bed!" She repeated his phrase with a show of impatience. "You're too complicated for the likes of us!" These words she spoke jokingly, but Gabriel detected a note of suffering in her voice. It was as though he were holding a pigeon in his hands and pressing it rather too tightly.

"My dear Mathilde, do you really expect me to believe that you're a simple soul?"

She rose with a quick movement:

"All this is just talk.... Do you remember that when you were a child my mother used to say that you were a great hand at talking nonsense? You go on ahead, I'll put out the lamps."

Suddenly the kitchen was empty of all light save what came from the dying fire. The copper pans caught a momentary flicker, and then went dim. Bergère's tail could be heard thumping the flagstones of the floor. The hall smelled of mold and linen. Cloaks and sunbonnets filled the great press. Gabriel turned sharply:

"And what about Catherine?"

"How do you mean—what about Catherine?"

Mathilde sounded cross. She spoke like someone in a hurry to get to bed.

"Is she happy?"

"Why shouldn't she be happy? What a question!"

"Have you asked her?"

"There's no reason why I should ask her. She has always known that this marriage was a foregone conclusion.... Not happy at the idea of marrying Andrès! Why, you must be crazy!"

"What is she like with him? How does she behave?"

"They do everything together, as they always have done. Really, you've become very stupid, my poor dear!"

They tiptoed up the stairs.

"Don't make a noise," she said: "Symphorien's a light sleeper; very different from Andrès. *He* wouldn't wake if the house fell down!"

"Is he still in the green room? Since there's no danger of waking him I'll just slip in and give him a kiss.... You coming?"

He was holding the door half open.

"Wait a moment," she whispered. "I'll light the bedside lamp."

The boat-shaped bed was hung with curtains printed in a design of red and green. At first, Gradère could see nothing but the huge, inflated eiderdown. The room was so stuffy that he could scarcely breathe. "How typical!" he thought. "Country folk never open their windows at night!"

"He's got too much on his bed," murmured Mathilde. "It's always been a mania with him ever since he was a child. I don't mind betting he's in a regular sweat," she added, taking off the eiderdown.

Gabriel looked at his sleeping son. The boy's face was flushed. A black smudge of beard accentuated the color in his cheeks. He was not wearing pajamas, but an old-fashioned hem-stitched night-shirt. His forehead was damp and caught the light. "The very image of his mother," thought Gabriel, "but in him it shows as good looks...."

Andrès stirred, and his hand felt for the eiderdown.

"In summer he goes to the opposite extreme," said Mathilde—she spoke with the fondness of a mother to whom everything that concerns her child has an exaggerated importance. "He can't stand anything on his bed, not even a sheet. Sometimes I have to cover him up, because even in August it's chilly about dawn, because of the stream..."

"Soon there won't be any need for you to bother...." Gradère had left the room. Moonlight drenched the staircase, making the handrail shine. But it could not penetrate the dark tunnel of the corridor.

"What a lovely night!" sighed Mathilde. "No need for candles. What was that you said?"

"I said that soon you wouldn't have to bother about covering Andrès up when the dawns are chilly.... He won't be alone." He was on the alert for Mathilde's answer, but failed to notice the slight change in her voice when she said:

"Yes, for the first few days after they're married I shall have to be careful not to go into his room.... It has become a habit with me."

"One's got to sacrifice something," said Gradère.

"Oh," she said with a laugh, "it won't be any sacrifice. I know only too well that I treat him like a little boy. It's time I stopped."

"He probably feels the same about it. I'm afraid you may get on his nerves a bit."

"Nonsense!" she protested sharply. "Actually, he's only just a child, even though he is twenty-two. His time in the army didn't change him a tiny bit. He's still very innocent, you know," she added hastily.

"How do you know?"

"I don't mean that he tells me things...but in some ways he is extraordinarily simple.... Odd, isn't it, with a father like you?"

Gradère fixed his blue eyes on her:

"Maybe it's you that are simple.... You're the last person in whom a young man of twenty-two would confide...."

She broke in on him:

"I said that because I am sure it's true. Don't, please, pretend to know better than me! Besides, at Liogeats nothing can be kept secret for long. If he'd ever had the least bit of an adventure, I should have heard of it the same day.... You can take my word for it that nothing of the sort has even so much as entered his head. People like you can't believe that there are men in the world who are not just animals, not just dogs!"

"How violent you are, Mathilde! I didn't mean to be offensive…"

"I don't find what you said in the least offensive—why should I?" She was furious. "Come, it's time we were in bed. We'd be much better off there than hanging about talking nonsense. Do you still prefer tea for breakfast?"

"No, not here. The water tastes of earth and limestone.… Coffee, please, the same as the rest of you."

A high pitched voice from the far end of the corridor made them start.

"You're talking too loud: you've woken Papa!"

"Is that you, Catherine? How long have you been there?"

Mathilde asked the question in a preoccupied voice.

The newcomer avoided the question.

"Papa heard you… Would you like me to give you a light?"

They blinked in the sudden glare. Gradère looked at the lanky girl. She seemed cold, and was wrapped in a dressing gown like her mother's, and made of the same purple material. Her face was dark and brooding, though there was in it a wary quality which gave her an animal expression, though it did nothing to lighten the hard, bony structure. Her thick, lusterless hair was arranged in two plaits and drawn back, revealing a low forehead. She was a true woman of the Landes, one of the little black hens peculiar to that countryside. Her mother looked at her anxiously.

"I suppose you thoroughly enjoyed listening to us, didn't you? Not that it matters in the least."

Catherine moved her shoulders in a faint shrug. She stared at her slipper which had a hole in it through which her big toe was projecting, and played with the faded ribbon of one of her plaits. Suddenly, addressing herself to Gradère, she said:

"Papa's expecting you tomorrow morning…as soon as you are up. He is very pleased that you have come."

"Are you pleased, too, Catherine?"

"Oh, I…"

Her gesture seemed to imply that what she felt was of no interest to anybody. Her diminished shadow melted into the gloom of the corridor. Mathilde and Gabriel waited until she had closed the door of her room, which communicated with her father's.

"Do you suppose she overheard what we were saying?" he asked.

"Probably—she's always hanging about…and spying. Her father has trained her to act like Bergère…." There was a note of hatred in her voice.

"A pleasant sort of wife for Andrès, eh, Mathilde?"

"Just the wife he needs!"

"True," he replied in dulcet tones: "she'll adore him; she'll be mad about him."

Mathilde flung him a dry "good night" and went into her room. Gradère heard the sound of the bolt being shot. He was still laughing when he entered his own room, which had once been Adila's.

A photograph of the dead woman stood on the mantelpiece, propped against a vase which Mathilde kept filled with roses. Gabriel had stopped laughing. He sat down on the bed and looked about him. There were some bad pastel portraits on the walls, done by old Grandpapa Du Buch, and two watercolors, one of Saint Bertrand de Comminges, the other of the Lac d'Oo. A number of religious images were scattered about the room—the Sacred Heart, the Virgin, St. Joseph, and a great brass crucifix on which was hung a rosary of olive stones which had been much valued by Adila because Pope Pius IX had blessed it.... For the second time that evening Gabriel felt at peace. He had never been conscious, in this room of Adila's, of that sense of bodily warmth, as of some invisible presence, which so terrified him in Paris; had never heard the breathing of someone on the watch. On a sudden impulse he got up, opened the wardrobe with the creaking door, took from the bottom shelf an old red flannel cape, and raised it, not to his lips, but to his nose. He had a way of sniffing at objects, like a dog. That done, he sat down again on the bed, holding Adila's red cape on his knees, clinging to this piece of flotsam with both hands. The moon went down, mist covered the fields. Every living creature at Liogeats, except only Gabriel Gradère, was fast asleep.

4.

SOMEBODY else was keeping vigil in the house that gleamed with a leper's whiteness, though his eyes were fast shut. The moonlight drifting through the slats of the Venetian blinds shone upon untidiness. The room was vast and scantily furnished. The truckle bed was of iron. On the table a scatter of papers showed like snow. What could those objects be upon the floor, looking like two motionless animals? Only a pair of heavy boots caked with mud. A flannel shirt and a soutane were draped over one of the chairs. Damp patches on the walls assumed in the moonlight the form of continents and islands. The Abbé Forcas could hear overhead the scampering of rats, a sound of gnawing, and an occasional faint squeal. He was thinking not of rats, but of the branches he had found upon his doorstep.... Why had he not shifted them? There was still time.

On the previous evening, while reading his Breviary, he had heard, beneath the windows, a noise of muffled laughter, and, creeping close, had seen and understood. He had been filled with the sort of mad rage which comes only to full-blooded fellows of twenty-six. It must be that lout Mouleyre who was responsible, or Pardieu, the wheelwright's son...probably egged on by the girls. There were two or three of the latter who hated the lonely young man round whom they snuffled in vain. He had rushed headlong down the stairs, had seized the latch, but then had checked his impulse. Regaining his room, he had knelt down as though his longing to sweep the doorstep clean had been a temptation. But surely it could not be called that? Was it not his duty to forestall a scandal which the return of daylight would reveal? "Did I fear scandal when I was stripped of My garments, bound naked to a pillar, nailed naked to a cross?... Not yours to understand, but to resemble Me." Alain Forcas reflected: "I was talking to myself," and at once the voice fell silent.

He had undressed in a fury, flinging the soutane from him. Then, he had picked it up again with reverence, and pressed it to his lips. At that moment, standing there, he was just a young man like other young men. He looked smaller than, in fact, he was, because he had a long body and short legs. The rather sullen face with its freckled nose and the low forehead of a young buffalo, spoke not of suavity but of violence....

In bed, he lay turned to the wall, his hands linked by his rosary. Should sleep not come at once, it couldn't be helped. He would get up and sweep the doorstep clear. Why must he always submit? He should have resisted the Dean, should have refused to send Tota away. What right had anyone to forbid him to give shelter to a sister who had been left forlorn and destitute? She had gone back to Paris well-nigh penniless. What sort of life was awaiting her there? "Rootless and lost" she had moaned in a low voice. He thought of the Dean: "a saint, but lacking bowels of pity—one of those who are born without them." His lips moved; at regular intervals he murmured a woman's name: *"Mary, Mary, Hail Mary...."*

He was once more like a little child burying its face in a shoulder. He closed his eyes because his mother was holding him tight.... Nothing else mattered to him but to be kept there, not to yield to his desire to go downstairs, to open the door, to sweep away the branches. It was a simple desire to which any man might have felt it his duty to surrender—any *other* man. But such a duty was not for him. He knew the nature of his mission: never to turn aside his head, never to make the gesture of refusal. In all other ways he had been a failure. Neither with the children nor with the old people would he find a welcome. Here, in this little town, it was not a question of apathy or ignorance, but of active hatred, which, in some, was virulent. He was looked on with a mistrust that had become deep-rooted during the ten years in which two lukewarm priests had held this curé of souls. The inexperience due to his youth had been exploited; his every fault of tact-lessness had been exposed to the full light of day; any feeling of affection he might have for one or other of his parishio-ners had been mocked, or attributed to base motives, until, with the arrival of his sister, the attitude of his neighbors had become one of definite persecution. "You have failed in whatever you have turned your hand to...you are incapable of doing anything except endure.... Endure, then!"

There might have been the children, the few children of Liogeats, but they had been taken from him on the very evening of their First Communion. Not one had he kept.

Which of them would willingly have been seen speaking to him? "What cause have you for complaint? Many are the priests who can find none to serve their Mass, whereas you have always little Lassus." He thought of the boy whose father was unknown, whose mother was in service at Bazas, who lived with an aunt. Very soon now he would be ringing the *Angelus*, and, as soon as the Abbé entered the church, the first thing he would see would be a pair of wooden clogs standing in the porch, and, close to the altar, a small, cropped head with projecting ears.

But before reaching the church he would have to tread upon those ignominious branches, and cross the Square, watched by malicious eyes—the eyes of those who lived like rutting goats, while he, at twenty-six, was all alone; alone in the daytime, alone in the evening, alone at night...one confession every fortnight. He must not stumble nor fall in the interval, if only because of his daily Mass...a Mass without listeners, a Mass said in a wasteland. "No, not wholly without listeners. The boy is there, making his responses; and sometimes the old aunt."

What was Tota doing at this moment? Was she asleep or still trailing about Paris? Those branches.... He would get up earlier than usual, so that no human being on the Square should witness his shame. After Mass, during the Thanksgiving, Lassus should sweep the presbytery doorstep.

Alain was breathing gently. Sleep had come at last. There was never anyone to watch him as he slept. He was a young man, like other young men, with a prematurely aged face and fresh lips—an unhappy child. But his consecrated hands crossed upon his breast made a patch of light in the dark.

The *Angelus*. And he had meant to get up at dawn! It was already full day. He would be seen, watched, as he left the house. He ran to the window and pushed open the shutters. God was good! A thick mist, shot through by the crowing of cocks, hid the earth. A wagon jolted by a bare stone's throw away, but he could not see it. The mist would cover him like the wings of God. *Scapulis suis obumbrabit tibi: et sub pennis ejus sperabis....* He would leave shaving till after Mass (though he was not one of those priests who have the effrontery to approach the altar uncleansed). He must hurry, so as to reach the church before the sun had dispersed the mist, before God had withdrawn His wing.

But the mist was already lifting when he opened the door, and, suddenly, he saw that the old stones, still wet with dew, were bare. Scarcely venturing to touch them with the soles of his shoes, he stood and stared. Not the trace of a leaf was anywhere near, not the least little twig.... But yes, there was *one*, lying between the steps and the wall, as though to assure him that he was not dreaming. He picked it up and crushed it between his fingers. Heavens! It must be young Lassus who had done this!

Alain Forcas reached the church without seeing a soul. Where the nave began, he said a brief prayer. At the sound of his steps the boy had risen from his knees, and now walked before him to the Sacristy. As a rule the priest did not speak to him before Mass. This morning he laid his hand on the cropped head, and smiled down at the thin, ill-nourished face.

"Haven't you had time to wash this morning, Jacquot?" The lad blushed and explained that he had been afraid of being late.

"I know what made you late."

Lassus told him that his aunt's alarm clock was out of order.

"But the real reason was that you had work to do outside the presbytery, wasn't it?"

What work? He did not know what Monsieur le curé meant. He hadn't been near the presbytery, but had taken the short cut through the Douences' garden...as he always did when he was behind time.

Then it hadn't been the boy! There must be one other person in Liogeats capable of pity! Some member of his flock had been moved by a feeling of compassion for him! "Maybe he will never reveal himself," he thought. No matter, this morning's Mass should be said for him. Thus thinking, he approached God's altar which, through every tribulation, was the stay and comfort of his youth.

He walked home slowly, because young Lassus' clogs were clacking at his side, and he had to shorten his stride in order to keep step. The boy was chattering away breathlessly. To hear him the Abbé would have had to lean down. But as yet he could not emerge from his sense of inner peace, from his spirit's silence. The coming day would be full of duties. He would try to visit all the sick of the parish. He fully expected to be welcomed no better than a dog, but he felt sufficiently strong now to bear the mistrust which would be his portion. It was only unexpected blows that made him feel afraid. He knew from experience that this lightness of heart after Mass concealed a threat, that somewhere a snare had been set. No use pretending: he had planned to visit the sick, not from any love of self-sacrifice, but so as to forestall the hidden danger.

Already his inner silence was ebbing, withdrawing, and life was seeping back from all sides. Not for a moment did he lower his guard, but remained on watch for the attack which might come he knew not whence. The branches had not been laid for nothing…the insult must be connected with something of which he did not know. He hurried across the Square. The schoolmaster was standing on the steps of the Mairie, deep in conversation with Dupart, the mayor's deputy. The Abbé raised his hat. Only the schoolmaster replied with a lift of his béret. Dupart said something in his ear, and laughed. Seeing the presbytery close at hand, the Abbé felt like a hunted fox when he comes within sight of his den. At that moment he heard the boy say something about Madame Revaux, which was the name of the sister whose presence here had been for him the cause of so much wretchedness.

"P'r'aps the bit about the hotel at Lugdunos *is* true. No less than three people did see her on market day.… But there be some as say as how you do go visiting her, and have been seen in ordinary clothes."

"Is all that gossip *still* going on?" muttered the Abbé, taking his key from his pocket. "Why, my sister is in Paris."

But even as he spoke the words, he remembered that she had not once written to him since her departure, and that he had no proof whatever of her having gone to Paris. What the boy had said might be true. On the other hand, what should she be doing all alone at Lugdunos?

"Here's a letter for you, sir," said young Lassus: "'twas slipped under the door.…"

The hand of innocence held out a yellow envelope to the Abbé.

Alain knew precisely what it contained, and might have torn it up without bothering to read what was written. As it was he stuffed it into his pocket, while the boy busied himself about making coffee.

He waited until he was alone before opening the envelope:

Tartufe! Everyone at Lugdunos saw you at seven o'clock on Friday, you dirty swine! Tual's commercial had the room next to yours. He may not have seen, but he heard!

More than once, as he read, the young priest paused and caught his breath. He felt as though he were suffocating in the stench that came from the letter in his hand. Then, with a deep sigh, he continued to the end.

5.

THAT night Mathilde was unable to sleep. Anxiety about Andrès' marriage and about the sale of Cernes and Balisaou, which was ever uppermost in her mind and regularly kept her awake, tormented her until dawn, but now other worries were added to it. The mental distress that comes with the hours of darkness is never simple, being composed and orchestrated, like a symphony, in a pattern of interweaving motifs. Had Catherine overheard her mother's conversation with Gradère? At what precise moment had the girl taken up her vantage point in the corridor? Mathilde tried to remember what it was she had said about her. "Was she already there when I cried out (because that is practically what I did do) that I thought her ugly, morose, sullen...did she hear all that? It would be horrible if she did." But that was not the worst. Though Mathilde had managed to disguise the distress which Gabriel's insidious words had caused her, she had lied to him. Andrès was *not* any longer in what is usually described as "a state of innocence." True, he had been for many years, and pretended to her that he was so still. But she knew well enough that he was playing a part whenever they were together. He still called her "Tamati" as in the old days when he had been unable to say "tante Mathilde." The very tone in which he spoke the word, the way he behaved like a spoiled child, were all of a piece with that baby language. She had remained "Tamati" to him but there were many things in his life now that Tamati could never know.

Nothing, to be sure, can long remain a secret in small country places, where all one's neighbors' actions are matters of common knowledge; but several times a week Andrès left the house at crack of dawn—giving as his reason that he had tree-felling to supervise or dealers to see—and was often away for forty-eight hours at a time. Symphorien Desbats, for all his stinginess, was generous in the matter of petrol. It was almost as though he *liked* to think of Andrès roaming the countryside. "But why?" Mathilde wondered.

There was no proof at all that Andrès was not, as he said he was, keeping an eye on the estate and visiting the farmers— with whom he was on very good terms (they were almost his only friends), or occasionally having a drink with old army pals. "That's all very well, but why has his appearance changed so suddenly in the last six months? I was always at him for looking so grubby and unkempt, and now he's begun to spruce himself up." Not for the first time, in that room of his which Gabriel found so intolerably stuffy, had she been conscious of a pervading scent of lotions, of the smell of stale hair-oil. What he most admired in his father was an appearance of elegance of which he quite failed to realize the shoddiness. The big, strong youth was dazzled by the old and worn-out buck…. Well, she reflected, he was, after all, his son, his and

Adila's and how could any child of theirs be wholly innocent? What reason had she for believing that Andrès was chaste or retiring? From far back he had derived from his father an idea of "woman" which had left him bitterly critical of the young females of Liogeats. Not one of them found favor in his eyes. For a long while this contemptuous attitude had been, with Mathilde, a matter for rejoicing. "Time enough for all that later on," she had thought. She knew now that they would never attract him. But that there was *some* woman in his life seemed almost certain. Who it could be she had no idea. She had always had "feelings" about him, and her feeling at this moment was that he was the victim of some obscure and overwhelming passion, though that did not alter the fact that he was planning to marry Catherine, that he looked on marriage with her as a foregone conclusion.

When Gabriel had questioned her about Catherine's and Andrès' attitude to one another, she had not known what answer to make, because it had been a rule with her never to think about it.... How did the boy behave when he was with Catherine? The fact was that he treated her like a sister for whom he felt no particular affection. No, not even that. It would be more accurate to say that he scarcely seemed to see her, that for him she was just part of the house, a piece of furniture that he had taken over with the rest of the property. He had grown up, had been trained, in the expectation of "inheriting" her, and his intention had never shown the slightest sign of weakening. Whatever else there might be in his life, it was not of a kind to deflect him from the projected marriage.

Mathilde heard two o'clock strike. She must get some sleep. She did not wish to carry her reflections further, being well aware that her thought had merely scratched the surface. But just as she would have scouted any temptation to indulge in scrupulous self-examination, so now she deliberately refused to explore her own responsibility in this matter of her daughter. Not one of Gabriel's insidious inquiries but had long lurked in the background of her mind. She had always avoided facing the issue. She made her confession once every month (rather less often now that she had felt compelled to go to the Dean because of the gossip that was making the rounds on the subject of the Abbé Forcas). What was not matter for confession could not be a sin. Why look for trouble? Catherine would be happier with Andrès than with anybody else. She could never have found a man willing to marry her except for her money. Of course, marriages between cousins…but it had never occurred to Mathilde that Andrès might have children. Perhaps there would never be any…

SHE awoke about eight o'clock, and dressed hurriedly. She recognized Andrès' step on the porch, and opened the window.

"Wait a moment," she called down to him, "and I'll join you."

There was not a breath of wind. The November sun was still warm. Light flashed from dew and puddles. Andrès declared that the fine weather would not last. He kept his gaze steadily on the windows of Symphorien's room, where the old man had been closeted with Gradère for more than an hour.

"I can't imagine what they've found to talk about all this long time," said Mathilde nervously. "They've been at it for ages. They can hardly be discussing the price because that's already been agreed upon.... Your father must be angling for a commission."

"No, Tamati; you're being unfair to Papa. Besides, it really doesn't matter. Cheer up: the question of my marriage has been settled once and for all."

"Are you positive?"

She took his arm and led him into the path that skirted the fields. She was in high spirits.

"All our land and all the Desbats coming to you! When I think of what sort of a man your father is, it's really more than we could ever have hoped."

"I won't have you running down Papa...."

They had come to a halt in the middle of the path. She studied him carefully. He was wearing a sports-coat ordered from *La Belle Jardinière,* and leggings. He was a dark-skinned young fellow, rather short and thickset. The expression of his face was open and smiling, but it had a way of turning sullen as the slightest word, so suspicious was he, so ready to believe that others were laughing at him. She noticed that he was freshly shaved, and had flattened down his naturally wavy hair. She smiled.

"Is it in honor of your father that you've smartened yourself up so? I suppose you want to compete..."

"When I'm with him I look like a country lout."

Mathilde bridled:

"Of the two of you he's the one who looks like a country lout...."

"But there's no resemblance between us—not the slightest."

"You little silly! You're far more truly elegant than he is.…"

"Poor Tamati!"

"You have the looks and the bearing of a boy of your class. There's a false air of smartness about him with his light suits.… He looks all wrong, somehow."

"I don't agree. Let's talk about something else…"

He walked ahead of her towards the house, kicking at a pine-cone and sulking. "I oughtn't to have said that," thought Mathilde. "After all, he *is* his father…but he knows nothing about him, whereas, I.… But why should I mind if he has illusions about Gabriel?"

She spoke again:

"I don't wish any ill to your father. The great thing is that you're not a bit like him.…"

He scowled at her:

"I'm a great deal more like him than you think!"

"No," she answered with a smile: "I'm quite easy on that score."

Words came from him in an ill-tempered mutter:

"My stupidity, my ignorance, have given you a wrong idea of me. I've never got out of my rut. Consequently, you think I'm no good for anything but keeping an eye on the felling, and doing accounts with the farmer…just about good enough, in fact, to marry Catherine.…"

Mathilde stopped dead, startled into immobility. "You're *not* going to make difficulties…not now, just when we're in sight of the goal?"

His hands were stuffed into his pockets, his shoulders hunched.

"No," he growled. "The whole business has been dragging on long enough. The sooner it's over and done with, the better. Don't worry."

She heaved a sigh of relief and took his arm. "Dear boy, there's something I want to say.... I realize that Catherine and you are old friends...all the same, you might be a little nicer to her. You don't, really, make any effort...after all, she *is* engaged to you...."

"What on earth are you getting at? Why should Catherine and I pretend to feel what neither of us does feel? Marriage won't make the slightest difference to our lives. Things will be put on a business footing as Uncle Symphorien always agreed that they should be, that's all. The whole thing's a mere formality...."

Never before had Andrès spoken so cynically, and Mathilde felt deeply shocked. It was not he, but his father who was speaking, his father, who had so strong an influence on him.

"But darling," she insisted: "you *must* think of Catherine a little. The poor child has got feelings like everybody else. I don't doubt for a moment that you'll make her an attentive and affectionate husband, but don't forget what you owe her. Marriage is a sacrament...."

"Oh, come off it! Catherine doesn't expect me to be anything more than a good man of business. I shall carry on with my job, only..."

Thoroughly disconcerted, Mathilde looked hard at him.

"...only, I shan't forget that for years the old man has been exploiting me, that I've worn myself out in his service, and got nothing, or next to nothing, for my pains.... I've a right to some sort of return, haven't I, Tamati?"

He *was* like his father. In a flash he had become the very image of him. Not for the first time she recognized the cajoling way in which Gradère, as a boy, had always masked a concentrated and ferocious greediness.... She was only too familiar with this particular phenomenon. A pink and white, sickly child had suddenly peeped out from the black-haired youth. This was no longer the Andrès she had known....

She was perfectly well aware that what he had said had not been said at random, that every word had been premeditated, and that Gradère had been his tutor.

"Yes, things'll be on a regular footing, from now on. I shan't, any longer, have to be constantly on the spot, studying the crops and keeping the old man in good fettle. I'm counting on being able to take a trip to Paris now and again to see my father. He's quite alone, he's got nobody. He's been exploited, too—it's my duty to look after him...."

"But, Andrès, your Uncle Symphorien can't possibly do without his daughter.... Catherine is indispensable to him...."

"We shan't quarrel over *her*," said Andrès with a laugh.

"But if you do go to Paris, it won't be for long, will it? You hate Paris, you know you do. You can't breathe when you're away from Liogeats."

"That's what *you've* decided. You always have decided what I like and what I don't like. I've no intention of leaving Liogeats. I shall go off from time to time, but I shall come back. It'll all depend."

"On what? On whom?"

He said nothing. His smile revealed strong, healthy teeth, unevenly spaced—his mother's teeth. On the face of the young man whom she had loved dearly ever since he was a child, Mathilde caught an expression that told of some vague desire now coming triumphantly into the open, though what its nature was she did not know. In a low voice, she said:

"And how about me, Andrès? What's going to happen to me?"

"Oh, Tamati," he replied teasingly: "it's no good your pretending that you haven't had full value from me up to now! Besides, I'll cook up a little grandson for you in next to no time…perhaps a couple…and I shan't quarrel over them, either. Besides," he added with a hint of malice in his voice, "you mustn't forget that you'll always have your daughter.…"

It wasn't like him to say that. Gradère was speaking through the lips of innocence.

The sun was already high and as hot as in late September. The cows were ambling, one by one, into the pasture, and, behind them, the farmer's boy was closing the gate all sparkling with dew. Mathilde riveted her attention on the animals. She did not want to know the nature of her feelings at that moment. She refused to see what was as plain as a pikestaff. Her whole will was concentrated on making this conversation no different from those other conversations she had had with Andrès. He was going to be a rich man. His father would get his hooks into him, would probably pervert him.… He would run away and see the world. It was just as simple as that.

But suddenly, as unexpected, as unintended, as a rush of blood to the mouth, a cry escaped her. It had been uttered even before she knew what she was saying.

"You don't love me! You never have loved me!"

He stared at her in amazement. She herself seemed shocked by her outburst. When next she spoke, she tried to be calmer, more light-hearted, but her voice was still trembling:

"What more could I have done for you if you had been my own son?"

"What more could you have done, Tamati? Do you really want me to answer that question? Well, in the first place, you could have thought about my future. You could have sent me away from this house where I was growing up to be just a country bumpkin. You could have decided that what the village schoolmaster could teach me wasn't enough. You could have sent me to a boarding-school in Bordeaux. What a hope! You were bored, living here with the old man. Your daughter Catherine…but we won't talk about her…. I was your distraction, your delight. Later on, you agreed that your husband should turn me into a sort of unpaid bailiff. Provided I stayed on permanently at Liogeats, you didn't bother. I had to have some amusement, so you thought of football, and coughed up a playing field. Oh, I know I'm the star performer of the village, and, naturally, if I hadn't had you…but don't try to make me believe that you've always treated me like a son… that's a bit too much!"

It was all true. Everything he was saying was true. Its truth came to her in a blinding flash. But who had opened his eyes? After all, she did know him through and through. This vague feeling that he had been sacrificed must have been implanted in his mind by somebody. Even the language he had used wasn't his own. Could it be that his father had prompted him? Then suddenly she realized. "It's some woman who has told him of all that he has missed…."

Though she knew that what he had said was true, she made an effort to justify herself:

"You're being unfair, dear. I *did* try to make you work but you never took easily to books. You used to say that you didn't need all that amount of learning to fit you for what you would have to do when you were a man.... The only things you liked were football, shooting, and riding."

"All young people talk like that, but most parents don't take it seriously. I should have learned to like reading. I'm no stupider than most young men of my age.... Merely because I organized a local football team. It was you who convinced me in the long run that I was brainless. Don't think I don't know my limitations. I'm no high-flyer, still..."

It never occurred to him that she had heard the last few words of the sentence, because he had spoken them as though to himself: "Still, I've got the gift of charming people...." But she had guessed his meaning.

She half turned her head away. He saw that she was crying, and tried to take her in his arms, because, really, he was very fond of her. Very quietly she freed herself.

"Please leave me alone. Go and see whether your father is still with Uncle Symphorien. Call me when they come out."

She watched him walk away, then looked around with pensive gaze. Scarcely anything had changed since the days of her childhood. The pines seemed to be less thickly planted, for many of them had died. The plantations had grown larger. But the smell of mist, the muted sounds of the late autumn morning belonged to as far back as she could remember. She had lost all sense of the passage of time. She felt as though she were a little girl again, running, out of breath, among the trees with Gabriel in pursuit, and her sunbonnet, fastened by an elastic round her neck, flapping up and down upon her shoulders in the wind of her scurrying course…Gabriel.…

She had tried, as she grew up, to think as little as possible about the past; never to dream or speak of it, but to live in the present, worrying only about what she could see and touch. Only the presence of the boy Andrès had made it possible for her to live up to that resolution. He was right. She *had* made use of him: *had* lived on his life. He had been to her as a pet dog, he, the son of the man she had once loved. She could never have faced life at Liogeats had she had no companions but Symphorien Desbats and Catherine. That was why she had never so much as considered sending him away to school. It was true. She had not watched over his education, had never tried to, but had done everything in her power to strengthen his passion for the land. So strong, she had felt, would be the feel of the land in his blood, that he would never want to leave Liogeats.… The sound of Andrès feet upon the stone steps reached her ears distinctly. She looked at the trees about her, and saw them as dead things. The hedges, the gate, the fields beyond, were to her as objects in a mirage, unreal as memories. "Lay not up for yourselves treasures." What a poignant meaning those simple words can take on for certain people at certain times. The clutching fingers relax their hold upon the branch. One no longer clings to anything.

The thought held her there motionless. For twenty years she had been living, without knowing it, in despair. Despair may become an unconscious state of mind. She leaned against an oak, listening, without taking it in, to the sound made by a passing wagon. For a very long time she did not move.

6.

ANDRÈS was calling to her from the steps. He was waving a paper, and she realized that the business was settled. It could only be at Catherine's expense. Once again she had to struggle with a vague feeling of remorse. Still, after all, the girl was not alone. Her father loved her as much as it was possible for him to love anybody (which was not saying a great deal). He had probably seen to it that she should not be sacrificed.

A remnant of curiosity made her hurry. Andrès ran towards her.

"It's all settled," he called out. "I've signed the deed of sale. It's in the form of a gentleman's agreement. Now we needn't think of anything but the marriage. Here's the text of the contract. It seems perfectly fair to me. All we want now is your approval."

He was breathing hard, and his face was flushed. He looked excited and happy. Mathilde glanced over the paper. The contract provided for a monthly payment to Catherine of ten thousand francs. Andrès was to have a percentage of the resin yield, and of all prices fetched by the sale of timber.

It was further stipulated that any expenses the young couple might have in setting up house should be defrayed, and that there should be no question of their paying an annuity. Andrès was to contribute all the property that remained to him to the common fund—one half of the house and garden (which had been jointly held since Adila's death).

"Nunky insists on opening a bottle of Champagne in honor of our betrothal. But his asthma's come on again badly."

Even before they had opened the door they could hear the wheezing of the sick man's breathing, and could catch the smell of eucalyptus. His was the smallest room in the house, and the air in it was always thick with the steam of fumigations. The invalid was sitting huddled in an armchair. He fixed a pair of glittering eyes on Mathilde and Andrès.

"All this emotion has brought on one of my crises," he gasped.

He was wearing a woolen waistcoat over his nightshirt. An eiderdown was tucked about his knees. It was popularly said that Catherine was the image of her father, though, truth to tell, all that Symphorien Desbats had in common with her was the purely animal expression of her face. Like her, however, he was small of stature and dark of skin. Everything about him was angular—his nose, the shape of his skull, his elbows and his bony shoulders. He was panting.

"You've read over the agreement, Mathilde? The sale's all fixed, and we've signed. Cernes and Balisaou are to come to me.... Balisaou and Cernes.... But I've shelled out for them, you know. The boy had to have ready cash for the engagement ring and a few odds and ends...not that they'll have much in the way of expense.... Gercinthe has gone down to the cellar to fetch the bottle of Roederer I've been keeping…as I've often told you…for Catherine's engagement…."

Gradère was on his feet. He looked rather flushed, and his eyes were fixed on the sick man. He made a sign to Andrès and whispered something in his ear. Gercinthe came in, carrying a bottle of Champagne and some glasses on a tray. Suddenly, Gabriel spoke:

"We're all here except the heroine of the occasion."

Symphorien glanced round him:

"That's a fact; 'pon my word…. Gercinthe, go and fetch Catherine…she can't be far away."

A fit of coughing shook him. His eyes never left the communicating door.

"Ah, there you are, m'dear…you were the only thing we'd forgotten."

The assumed look of surprise with which Catherine asked what all the excitement was about, and then her expression of terror, her cry—"I'm not engaged to anybody!"—were on the level of third-rate melodrama. Symphorien, on the other hand, was playing his part to perfection. He turned to Andrès with a look of bewilderment.

"But I thought you two had everything fixed up between you, my boy. You gave me your word that it was so…Catherine, why have you left me in the dark like this?"

Andrès had gone white and his lips were trembling. He looked in turn at his father, at Catherine, at Mathilde. Once again the dry, indifferent tones of the young girl broke the silence:

"You never asked me what I thought. I am engaged to nobody. I will never consent to marry Andrès."

Old Desbats was no longer bothering to keep up the farce. In spite of the asthma that was torturing him, his expression was one of profound satisfaction, with a hint in it of fear.

"My darling girl, no one's going to put pressure on you.... You're perfectly free, and..."

Gabriel broke in on him:

"Oh, lay off...this play-acting's gone on long enough!"

"My dear fellow, I don't know what you mean by play-acting. No one could be more surprised, more shocked than I am...I'd been building on this...I'm still hopeful that she'll think again"—and then, as Catherine interrupted the flow with "I've done all the thinking necessary," the next words came tumbling from his lips—"in any case, I shall stand by everything I've promised Andrès...."

The young man who, so far, had said nothing, and seemed stunned, now stammered out:

"You don't think, do you, that I shall stay here a day longer? I've slaved and..."

His father interrupted him:

"Don't talk nonsense, my boy. This house is yours, and you'll remain in it. You've been robbed, you've been plundered...but the chateau is partly yours. This is your home, and, since you've been so kind as to offer me hospitality, I shall stay too, for as long as may be necessary."

He kept his blue eyes fixed on the invalid, who was now hanging his head, but still watching him slyly.

"Necessary for what?"

Gradère replied without any show of emotion:

"For making you cough up..."

"Look here, my good fellow. If it comes to coughing up…
you've got a pretty good cheek, I must say…I hope you're not
going to force me to dot my i's…I'm perfectly ready to tear
up the deed of sale on condition that Andrès pays me back.…
But perhaps you've already disposed of your son's money?"

Only Gradère and Andrès heard these last words. The
young man took his father's hand. The latter had gone white
and now replied with dry finality:

"What's been signed has been signed."

There was a silence, which was broken by Mathilde
saying in a colorless voice:

"Ever since this engagement was first mooted, I, too, my
girl, thought that you and Andrès were in agreement. There
was a time when you used to speak of it yourself. But I shall
put no pressure on you.…"

The girl replied insolently that her mother had good
reason not to give herself that trouble. Mathilde shrugged her
shoulders, and, without saying another word, left the room,
followed by Gabriel and Andrès.

For a moment the sick man and Catherine sat listening.
He asked her to go and see whether the others were still lurk-
ing in the passage. She half opened the door—no, they had
disappeared.

"I hope, my child, that you see now the wisdom of what
I told you. It never does any good to irritate people. I suppose
you wanted to see the look on their faces. Well, you've had
your little bit of fun…and so have I, I don't deny it…but now
you heard what Gradère said? We shall never be rid of him."

"What of it?" asked Catherine, arranging the sick man's
pillows.

He groaned:

"Don't you realize there's nothing he would stick at?"

"How can he hurt us?" the young girl exclaimed loudly.

"Speak lower!" he whispered: "you don't know that man. I found out a good deal about him, and I've not told you half of it. You're not old enough, you wouldn't understand...." He shuddered. A tender smile lit up Catherine's unattractive face. She laid a hand on her father's forehead.

"He may be a bad lot, but he can't eat us! So far as I can see it's *we* who have the whip-hand of *him*"—there was a note of savage joy in her voice.

"I'm ill, Catherine, though not so near to dying as they think—and hope.... But I shall never shake off this asthma, though it may go on for years, of course. Clairac told me so, only yesterday.... But that doesn't alter the fact that I am utterly defenseless...." He broke off, struggling for breath: "Take care, child. I don't know what they're plotting.... Keep your eyes skinned so long as *he's* here. Sooner or later he'll go. There's someone in Paris who'll make him go back.... He's no idea that I've been corresponding with that precious Aline of his. Luckily, she's got a hold over him. All the same, I shall breathe a good deal easier when he's gone."

"Did you notice Mamma?" asked Catherine suddenly. "She's tough, all right: she never batted an eyelid. I was watching her the whole time...."

He hadn't, he said, been able to see her, because she had kept behind his chair.

"I'm not sure," said the girl, "that she isn't really rather pleased at my refusing to have anything to do with Andrès...."

She sat staring in front of her.

"It's not your mother you need to worry about…it's that ruffian…. I don't like it when he speaks softly. Keep an eye on everything, my girl… and especially on the kitchen…. Beware of fire, and don't go out after dark…."

A fit of coughing stopped him:

"And you'd better have a look at Andrès' accounts. His father was a tenant farmer, and, if it comes to the point, he'll always back his people against me. They say he loves the land, but it's an odd sort of love that makes a man stand in with those who eat us out of hearth and home! Besides, you've only got to see how he acquiesces in his father's robbing of us…. Little by little he's let all the rents fall into arrears…. He's as weak as water…. A fine state of affairs it'd have been if he'd come to be master here. Watch him well, that's all I've got to say…."

"Don't worry: I'll watch the lot of them."

7.

◈

"Has Andrès calmed down?"

"Yes, he's lying on his bed, and his eyes are shut. I've put a damp towel on his forehead."

Scarcely an hour had passed since Desbats had laid his cards on the table. Very quietly Mathilde closed the door of the room which she always thought of as "Adila's," though Gabriel was now occupying it.

"I always knew that Andrès had a temper," she said. "Since he's been grown up there have been times when I've seen him in such a blind fury that he carried on like a madman. But I've never known him to behave as he did just now. Obviously, he's taken it hard…."

She sat down on the bed. Gradère was smoking, his hands in his pockets, his lips a hard line.

"What really surprises me," went on Mathilde, "is that he seems so *unhappy* about it all. Anger's one thing, but he's genuinely suffering. I do believe he loves the place as he might love a person. To look at him now, one would almost suppose he'd lost someone he was fond of."

"You talk more truly than you realize."

She threw him a questioning look.

"And you're always saying you know him. My poor Mathilde, I can see a great deal further than you, and I've been here only since yesterday evening."

His words hurt her. It was not so much that they hinted at some frightening secret in the part of Andrès' life that was hidden from her, as that they proved to what extent this man had the boy's confidence. That very morning, while she lay asleep, he had told his father things that she had never known. With an air of detachment, she said:

"Oh, there's quite a lot I suspect!"

She was lying. She had not the slightest idea what he meant. He could see that she was suffering, and the knowledge that that was so made him suffer in his turn, though not from sympathy. In this very room that had once been Adila's, twenty years ago, he had let her peep behind his mask. She had discovered the sort of man he really was. He remembered the dull sound that her body had made as it struck the floor when she had fainted in the passage outside the door. And now it was for Andrès that she was in torment. Not that he was jealous of Andrès. But he would have liked to share with Mathilde the bitter memory of what once had been…. And now, everything, even bitterness, was dead in her. It was the knowledge of this emptiness that had got on his nerves, that had made him cruel to her. He watched her suffer, yielding to the curiosity, which the sufferings of others always roused in him, so that he longed to fan the flames. He pretended to have been taken in, he said:

"Naturally, you're far too sensitive not to have noticed that there is some woman in Andrès' life."

"I knew it!"

Her wide-open eyes were on Gabriel's lips.

"Then it will be no surprise to you when I say that none of *us* matter a rap to him. He's not my son for nothing! It's from me he's inherited that invincible determination to get what he wants, no matter at what cost.... He's just a bundle of instincts, like his mother was...."

She broke in on him:

"How dare you speak of Adila like that! How dare you mention her name!"

This defense of Adila was the pretext she needed in order to give free rein to her jealousy and her torment. But Gradère would not let the subject drop:

"You can't alter facts. Andrès is a child of love."

"No," she protested: "not of love, but of hate, because you hated Adila, just as she hated the fact that she had been victimized by you, enslaved and possessed by evil. Poor Andrès! A child of love, you say. You should say, rather, a child of hatred and remorse...."

"Oh, come now, Mathilde! I always thought big words were suspect in Liogeats. I find it difficult to recognize myself from your description, I, the 'aimless chatterer.'"

Had she heard him? She was sitting very erect, her hands crossed on her dark dress that was devoid of all adornment. What nobility there was in her forehead, in the line of brow and nose! But it was in the large mouth with its bloodless lips, in the ruined glory of her neck, that all her ardor and her torment showed. For a while she was silent, then, at last, she spoke:

"I know nothing of the woman Andrès loves—not even who she is. There is no one at Liogeats…"

"She's not a native of Liogeats. She was staying for a few weeks at the presbytery."

"You can't mean that creature!"

"He met her by chance one Thursday, in the train, on his way back from a rugby match at Saint-Clair. It was she who made the running. All through the autumn they used to meet in lonely paddocks and empty farmhouses. Now she's living over at Lugdunos, in that new hotel on the Place Malbec."

He could not take his eyes from her. He was amazed at her immobility (only a muscle at the corner of her lips twitched just perceptibly), at the calm way in which she put her next question:

"What possible connection can there be between this adventure of Andrès—which really has nothing to do with me—and his broken engagement?"

"Tota Revaux (that's her name) has recently left for Paris. It's common knowledge that she was at Lugdunos, and though her brother was entirely ignorant of her movements, gossip has it that it was he who arranged it all, that they're not even related.... You know better than I do the horrible tittle-tattle that goes on in Liogeats. She adores her brother, it seems, and that's why she has gone away, in spite of Andrès. She was afraid her staying on here might harm the Abbé. The boy accepted her decision because it was his intention, once the marriage was an accomplished fact, or perhaps even before, to join her in Paris...to set her up there.... But now all that's been blown sky-high.... I don't, personally, think that the woman's feeling for him is altogether disinterested, though he swears it is...."

Here, Mathilde interrupted him with the information that Andrès had recently received a fat cheque in connection with the sale of Cernes and Balisaou.... Gradère averted his gaze but said nothing. She went close to him.

"You did take that money from him, didn't you? Don't deny it."

He protested, but without any very great show of vehemence:

"Certainly not...he's merely invested it.... I'm giving him five percent on what he can't place elsewhere. I offered him every penny I had left, but he refused, because it wouldn't have been of any use to him. Besides, I've something better to offer...when he's in a fit state to listen. He's already promised me not to clear out until we've won our little game."

Mathilde trembled. She hated this soft voice of his: it filled her with a sense of horror that defied all analysis. She touched his shoulder, and then quickly withdrew her hand.

"It would be a great deal better if you were to clear out, too, Gabriel"—she spoke with sudden warmth, and on a note of supplication. "Go, leave me. Catch the three o'clock train...."

"My dear girl, I've got a lot of things to see to here."

She was insistent:

"You can only do harm. Whatever happens, it's no use your counting on me."

She was close to the door. He was still standing by the window, with his back to the light. She could see nothing but the outline of his face.

"You know, my dear, I can be very useful to you. You'll live to thank me...just see if you don't."

"No!" she protested. "No!"

"It would be wiser to find out what's in my mind before you say no. Have you any idea what it can be?"

She raised a finger to her lips and was listening intently: "I hear the car," she said.

"He's off to see *her*. Perhaps it's to be their last meeting...."

A cry escaped Mathilde:

"If only she doesn't take him with her!"

Gradère advanced towards her. She made no move, but stood there with her hand upon the latch. He took her by the shoulders.

"Don't worry. He'll obey me! I, too"—he went on with a false air of jollity—"am fond of the boy. Do you want me to abandon him in the middle of a crisis?"

In a low, harsh voice, he added: "He's going to be master here, and that before many weeks are out.... You can take my word for it!"

Still she said nothing, and he murmured, pressing her slightly to him (she could smell his breath):

"He is going to be master, because you are going to be mistress...."

She wrenched herself free:

"I count for nothing here, as you very well know. Desbats shares the throne with nobody."

"Of course, of course...but though asthma may not seem a very serious thing, my dear, it does in the long run put a considerable strain on the heart."

"He'll live to bury the lot of us: that's what Clairac says."

"I've a good deal more confidence in my diagnosis than in Clairac's."

He laughed. Such horror came over her at the sound that she felt strong enough to break the spell and leave the room. She went downstairs, crossed the hall, took a cape, and plunged into the mist which the midday sun was gilding but could not penetrate. The *Angelus* was sounding. Young Lassus must be ringing it. Ear-splitting sirens were screaming of freedom to the factory workers. She felt a lightness as of deliverance. Her sense of suffering had passed. The world was all a glow of light. Life had a taste of sweetness on her lips, a scent in her nostrils that she had long forgotten.... She was relying on she knew not what. She would wait for the morrow. The man she had just left had inoculated her with hope.

8.

ON the evening of that same day, the shutters remained open even though darkness had fallen. A street lamp on the Place Malbec at Lugdunos threw its light upon the bed where Tota lay stretched at full length, as under a shroud, smoking. She was watching Andrès gesturing. Standing there, at the moment of departure, he showed as no more than an overgrown and ill-dressed boy, a rugby player with a thatch of curly hair on a rather brutish-looking head. He, meanwhile, had eyes only for the movements of her lovely arm in the half-light, as she stretched it to the ashtray, or carried the cigarette to her lips.

"No," she said firmly: "you're not to use my brush!"

He obeyed at once, for he felt towards all her precious objects of ivory, her crystal bottles with their golden stoppers, a species of reverence. Looking at the low forehead with its crown of curls, she was thinking: "I should have got most awfully bored...." But what, then, was she to do—trot back to the fold, as Alain wanted; go and live at La Benauge—the house where her mother had died a year ago—and eke out an impoverished existence (the cellars were filled with wine—three years' gathering—still unsold; the vineyards were let to an unscrupulous wretch who cut back the plants so unmercifully that soon they'd be no good at all)? Death would be better than that! But how could she live in Paris on an income of twelve thousand francs? She might, of course, pick up somebody...but, for Alain's sake, she did not want to cut completely loose, to sink altogether into the mire. The only other possibility would be to follow Alain's other suggestion, and make it up with her husband—that drug addict, that semi-lunatic, who beat her...that poor fish who had never amounted to anything as a writer, or as anything else, if it came to that.... No, never! What she'd really like would be for Andrès to pay her occasional visits in Paris, and help her to make ends meet. After all, she did "like" him. She'd better get busy and make up his mind for him....

"I've got to think seriously about going back...for my brother's sake. I bring him nothing but trouble...."

"Who are you going back *to*? Come on, out with it!"

The collar of his shirt was open. She could see the full column of his powerful neck, the dark chin jutting slightly forward.

"There's no one, I tell you...and until I'm driven by sheer necessity there won't be anybody.... What's to stop you from going with me? Oh, I know all about your engagement...but you can easily cook up some story...."

He just perceptibly leaned towards her. A hand touched his lips. He collapsed into a chair like a felled tree.

"Are you crazy?"

He scrambled to his feet. She could hear the sound of his breathing.

"Tota, I *can't* go with you...."

No, it was utterly impossible. He remembered the instructions which, no longer ago than that very morning, his father had conveyed in a low voice as they had walked up and down the corridor after their interview with old Desbats: "Stay here: hang on for a few weeks and you'll be master. Then you can have this woman you say you can't live without. It entirely depends on you whether or not you lose her forever...."

Even at the height of the crisis which, a few moments later, had flung him sobbing and screaming onto his bed, those words had remained vivid in his mind, until, gradually, the thought of them had helped to calm him. Certain promises made by his father had about them an aura of mysterious solemnity. Impossible to resist the mere force of that affirmation. No, Andrès could not go with Tota. At all costs he must make her put off her own departure. He sat down again on the bed.

"Wait just a few more days. You promised you would, only an hour ago."

She looked at him with a secret feeling of disgust. She found him pleasing only in the dark, for then he became a faceless animal, incapable of exacerbating her by looking loutish and low...a decapitated body in the dusk.

"The mere fact that I can't make up my mind to go ought to convince you that there is nobody...I'm free to choose whether to go or stay.... There's no one waiting for me and if it weren't for Alain...."

Again Andrès said: "Then you're not in love with anybody?"

"The only person I love is in another life."

"Dead?"

"Worse than dead...a prisoner."

Like a child who takes everything literally, Andrès asked: "Do you mean he's in prison?"

She sighed:

"If he were in prison I could write to him. I should know that he was thinking of me as I was thinking of him. But to say that the walls of his presbytery, that the folds of his soutane, shut him away and isolate him, is less than half the truth.... We are infinitely distant from one another...."

"Oh, I get it! You're speaking of your brother!" He broke into a loud, happy laugh, and put his left arm about the young woman's shoulders.

"You gave me an awful fright, you know!"

The white stillness of her face drew him like a magnet. Slowly he approached his own. A car drove across the Place Malbec. Dogs barked. There was the sound of a horse moving at a walk. The trap stopped at the door. They could hear somebody talking patois in the dark. Not yet did Tota feel herself far enough away from her brother. Once again she would plunge into the murk which gave her the sense of being out of his reach—hidden from everything that a man like Alain could do to act upon a human creature by enveloping her in a vast network of prayer and suffering. But Andrès said he must go home. It was essential that his father should not think that he had taken to his heels. Why, she asked, should his family be more suspicious this evening than at other times; He answered evasively. On a note of urgency he said:

"You won't go away, will you?"

She stroked his hand without replying.

"Perhaps," she said at length, "it'll be enough if I move a bit further off.... I might settle down in Bordeaux...but you'll have to help me...I'm far from rich...."

He seemed put out. Just a little peasant, thought Tota, with his mind on his money bags. But he was remembering his father's promise: "Hang on for a few weeks, and the game's yours...." He insisted on her staying at Lugdunos. She did not absolutely refuse. Once more she seemed to belong to him, to be submissive to his will.

In vain he said again—"I'm going; I really must go...." He stood there, undecided, by the edge of the bed, and, because she was lying down, he looked to her enormous, though he was far from being anything of the sort. Once more she raised an arm that appeared to have no connection with her body, to be a poised reptile, her hand its head. She laid the palm against the boy's lips, and did not cry out when he gently bit her. A silence hung over the little hotel. The sound of chopping from the kitchen scarcely broke it.

"It really is goodbye this time," he said.

Once more their faces drew together in the darkness. She listened as his footsteps died away. She was in the habit of playing a game with herself which consisted in trying to keep the sound of them, and the roar of the car, within her hearing until the last possible moment. She could tell from the way his horn sounded near or far whether he had turned the corner by the cemetery or had gone onto the Saint-Clair road…. This evening, therefore, she could not fail to catch his rather heavy tread muffled by the carpet of the corridor…. Suddenly, she heard the dull sound of a fall, of a body crashing to the ground, of Andrès' voice shouting an oath, of a gurgle of laughter.

Tota leaped from her bed, groped for her dressing gown, and went out into the shadowed passage which was lit only by the glow coming from the staircase well. A huddle of bodies was struggling on the landing. Some joke must be going on: somebody was being held down by two guffawing youths who had flung a sheet over him.

The young woman was wearing scarcely any clothes, and dared not move forward into the light. The heavy laughter reassured her. But the man struggling on the floor fought free of the shroud in which he had been enveloped. She saw Andrès' face emerge, bleeding and contorted with anger. The two youths who had held him pinned to the carpet looked utterly bewildered. "Good Lord! Monsieur Andrès!"

Spattered with blood, he growled out: "Mouleyre? Pardieu? You swine! You couple of louts!"

By this time Tota had run to him. Kneeling by his side, she raised his head. The damage was not great. He was bleeding from the nose, and his upper lip was slightly swollen.

"Don't stand there," she commanded in a low voice. "Help me to get him into my room."

They were thoroughly upset. Andrès was one of themselves: he was popular: he never put on side, was a damn good footballer, and the best "forward" for miles round. But for him the Liogeats team would not have existed.

Fortunately, the hotel was almost empty at that time of

the year. The rooms on this floor were unoccupied. Mouleyre mumbled in his atrocious accent:

"He'll be all right.... We didn't know it was him. We were after playing a trick on the curé...just a bit of a joke!"

Andrès had been lying full length on the bed. Now he sat up and said:

"Nothing wrong with me."

The youths kept on saying: "We didn't know...really we didn't."

He shouted to them to clear out:

"And don't get talking. If you do I shall go to the police."

Mouleyre offered to stay behind in order to drive the car in case Monsieur Andrès was feeling tired. Pardieu could get himself home in the van. Of course they wouldn't breathe a word. But Andrès was still in a bad temper. "Get out, both of you!" he said.

Tota, who had not uttered a word while she was look-ing after Andrès, spoke at last. Without looking at the young men, she said:

"At least you can bear witness that the curé...." They gave her a sly look. It was Pardieu who answered, though he waited until he was in the corridor before doing so:

"Bear witness to what? What does it prove? It proves...."

He raised two thick fingers, one on each side of the béret that was drawn tightly over his narrow head.

Andrès tried to fling himself at them, but Tota restrained him.

"Let me get at them!"

They waited until the sound of the van had died away. This time it was the young man who lay on the bed, Tota who hurriedly dressed herself. The electric light filled the room with a harsh radiance.

"Why are you putting on your clothes? Aren't you coming back to bed?" He spoke as though he were begging a favor.

She said nothing, but opened the wardrobe and pulled out a mass of dresses and underclothing.

Andrès sat up.

"Are you mad? There's no train at this hour."

She said that she would take the morning one—at five-forty. She would lie down on the bed fully dressed until it was time to start. When he asked her where she was going, the only answer he could get was "As far as possible from here."

But she would write, she said, as soon as she had found somewhere, so that he might join her. He felt that she would have promised anything in order to get rid of him. His every supplication dropped dead against the blank wall of her silence. It was as though she was no longer there.

9.

❖

"I think I hear the car."

Gradère went to the door, opened it and listened. The light of the moon was softened by the mist. The world was silent save for the gurgling of the Balion swollen by recent rains. Mathilde had not left the chair in which she was sitting by the fire. Had it been Andrès, she would have known it beyond all possibility of doubt. She murmured: "We shall never see him again."

Gradère shrugged:

"He's been delayed.... Put yourself in his shoes.... But he's not a nitwit."

Mathilde got up suddenly:

"This time it is Andrès!"

Gabriel remarked that he could hear nothing. But already the sound of a car, emerging into life from the heart of silence, was coming closer.

"I can hear him changing down. He's just turned into the avenue."

Andrès came into the room and took off his shabby old

goat skin coat. He seemed not at all surprised to find them standing there at midnight.

"Darling!" exclaimed Mathilde. "You've hurt yourself! Your lip's all swollen, and what's that lump on your forehead?"

He explained that he had banged his face in the garage. It was nothing, he said. He crossed to the fire without answering their questions, merely remarking that he was hungry. Mathilde had had some soup kept hot, and now busied herself with laying the table. He sat down and started to eat noisily, as though he were at an inn. Gabriel, at some little distance from the table, went on smoking. Never once did he take his eyes from his son's face.

Mathilde, on the contrary, saw to his requirements but did not look at him. It came to her that she felt no wish to kiss him. The sight of him filled her with a sense of horror.

"And now, dear, it's time you were in bed."

He emptied his glass of wine at a gulp, and drew his chair to the fire. He was slightly flushed: there was a viscous look about his eyes, an ugly expression in the line of his lips. His injuries gave him the appearance of a naughty boy who had been in a fight.

"I'm not sleepy," he said: "besides, there's no time to lose. We've got a lot to discuss—unless, of course, you're tired...."

"Speaking for myself," broke in Gabriel, "I don't know the meaning of the word sleep—never have, since I started turning night into day.... *You'd* better go to bed, though, Mathilde: you're half asleep already."

She began to protest, but he gave her a look, the meaning of which clearly was "leave us alone."

She did not want to do any such thing, having no idea what this man was going to say to Andrès, but feeling convinced that the boy would need someone to stand by him. At the same time, she knew herself to be incapable of resisting Gradère's wishes. She was, as it were, in a plot with him. Everything would come out all right... though the cost might be high. Still, what had she got to fear? Nothing. All the same, she hesitated about leaving the room, and made no further move until Gabriel pushed her gently towards the door.

"Impossible to say anything with you here"—he murmured.

"What about?"

"You know perfectly well what I'm going to say."

She made a gesture to the effect that she did not know what he meant. He shrugged, and nodded his head in the direction of Andrès, who was sitting with his back towards them, his legs stretched out to the blaze.

Her shake of the head was barely perceptible. He opened the door and stood back to let her pass. She made one last effort to turn back.

"No, Gabriel," she brought out in a firm voice. "I *don't* understand."

He walked over to his son who had covered his face with his two roughened hands—"to keep the heat of the fire off," Gabriel thought at first. But, a moment later, he realized that the boy was crying.

"Don't mind me," he said. "We can have our talk later."

Andrès blew his nose noisily. He was shaken by sobs, as in the old days after one of his childish fits of temper. Bergère laid her muzzle on his knee and gazed up at him. "Better let him quiet down," thought Gabriel. He would wait until the boy was in a fit state to listen. There was no hurry; they had the night before them. Though he did not yet know how he was to begin, he had a strong feeling that he would carry the day, convinced, as he was, that he was being directed and supported by something outside himself.

"Well," he said, taking Andrès' hand and pressing it.

"She's gone."

"All the better. Yes, I mean that. All the better. She's leaving us a free field in which to get things here straightened out."

"I don't know where she is."

"In Paris, old man. That kind of bird always goes to roost in Paris.... Don't worry, we'll get her back for you. I don't mind betting there'll be a letter before the week's out...."

"She did promise she'd write..."

"Why those tears, then?"

The boy smiled. He suddenly felt full of hope again, and asked his father what news there was at the big house. Gradère drew up his chair, threw a log on the fire, and watched the flames as they leaped from twig to twig.

"Nothing, for the moment. We've got to think about the future, and a pretty near future at that. It's no good saying the old man's pretty far gone, that his heart won't hold out much longer."

"Is *that* what you're counting on?" said Andrès, breaking in. There was a note of disappointment in his voice. "And what about afterwards? Do you really think Catherine's likely to change her mind? I know her too well to believe that....

Besides, I wouldn't go through with it, not now...not for anything in the world."

He got up and started to move aimlessly about the room, saying over and over again, complainingly:

"If that's all you've got to suggest..."

"It's not a question of Catherine," said Gradère. "Oh, I don't deny that we might have tried it on when circumstances seemed favorable...but I realize that you're not prepared to overlook her attitude...especially since you can look forward to something a great deal better...." Then (in a lower voice): "By the terms of their marriage settlement—Tamati's and the old man's, I mean—all property subsequently acquired was to be held jointly. That means that, as a widow, she'll have the whole of her share of the Du Buch property, *plus* half of everything her husband got his hands on after they became man and wife—everything, in short, that he bought back off me."

Andrès was listening with his mouth half open and a frown on his forehead:

"A precious lot of good that does to me!" he muttered.

Gradère went on talking. His voice sounded quite color-less, as though he were discussing some purely academic point: "When it's a question of saving a patrimony, families will often agree to the oddest kind of pairings.... After all, there's scarcely any bond of relationship between Tamati and you: she was only your mother's cousin.... Naturally, it would have to be a marriage in name only—that goes without saying...then, once the business part of the affair was settled, things between you would be just as they are now...."

"You must be raving, Papa!"

121

Andrès bent down and shook his father's shoulder.

"You're completely crazy!"

"But why, if the thing remains just simply a matter of form? I realize, of course, that you couldn't marry anyone else during Tamati's lifetime…but you needn't make yourself miserable over that…and when, sooner or later you're free…"

"Well, but look here: in the first place, can you really see her lending herself to a mockery of that sort…matter of form or no matter of form? I know her. She looks on me as her son. She'd think such an idea monstrous!"

Gradère shook his head: "You're quite wrong," he said with a knowing laugh. "Take my word for it, she'll agree to everything. We've got plenty of time to prepare the ground.…"

"And what are the people of Liogeats going to say? Can't you just see their faces?" Gabriel remained unperturbed.

"The marriage," he went on, "can take place privately, though that may be a bit difficult with Catherine in the house. We shall have to give a little more thought to that side of it. As a matter of fact, where money's concerned, there's not much that folk hereabouts aren't prepared to swallow."

"But look here, Papa. What does all this amount to? Uncle Symphorien's perfectly hale and hearty.

"Hearty, perhaps…hale? I'm not so sure."

"Anyhow, he may hang on for years."

"You're dreaming, my good idiot!"

"Well, for a good long time, then…and I can't wait.… I refuse to go on living in this state of uncertainty!"

Andrès resumed his prowling. His father, who was following him with his eyes, said suddenly:

"You won't be in a state of uncertainty for long—I guarantee that."

Andrès stopped dead and stared at the man who had just spoken. The voice was the voice of a stranger. Gradère, seated on a low chair, his elbows on his knees, kept his face averted. All that Andrès could see of him was the almost slender back of a neck, and a pair of shoulders that looked thin beneath the heavy English tweed. He could hear the man's quickened breathing.

He took a few steps and opened the door giving on to the garden. The night was clean and cold. The gurgling of the Balion made one with the sighing of the faint breeze. He passed his hand over his forehead and turned back to face his father.

"Do you mean to say you can see into the future?" he said with a laugh. "That you know what's going to happen?" He had laughed in order to break the spell that was on him, to get himself back into the atmosphere of everyday.

The other, still leaning forward to the fire, replied:

"The future is what we choose to make it." At these words he raised his eyes to the young man, and was struck by the expression of anxiety and unease upon his face. "Why are you looking at me like that, Andrès? What have I said that's so extraordinary?"

"Nothing at all...."

The boy shook his head as though to chase away an absurd and hateful thought. Suddenly, the memory of Tota came back to him. For two or three minutes she had been absent from his mind, but now the thought of her came flooding in again, or rather, he was conscious of her as of a ball of fire deep in his being, mingled with all that was most himself....

Gradère, having said what he had to say, fell silent. There was nothing to do now except to wait.

The latch of the door leading to the stairs moved softly, and Mathilde came in. She had put on her purple dressing gown and plaited her hair for the night. They had not heard her because her bare feet were thrust into a pair of bedroom slippers. "I came down again," she said, "because I felt uneasy. Do you know what time it is?"

Andrès stared at her for the space of a few seconds only. There was an extraordinary intensity in his gaze. She said:

"What have you been talking about?"

"Hanged if I know. What *have* we been talking about, Andrès?"

The young man made a vague gesture and hurried from the room. Mathilde and Gradère followed him.

They climbed the stairs, all three of them, through the silent house. The wooden treads creaked beneath their feet.

As they reached the bedroom floor, a door opened and they saw a wavering shadow creep along the wall. A moment later, Symphorien Desbats stood before them, in his nightshirt, a terrifying image of emaciation.

"What have you three been plotting at this time of night? It'll soon be day."

Mathilde explained that they had been made nervous by Andrès' failure to return. She was sorry, she said, that they had wakened him.

But by this time the old man was screaming his head off:

"You're lying! I heard the car. Andrès got back ages ago! I want to know what you've been up to!"

Gradère interrupted him, speaking loudly: "So now we mayn't even talk! That's the latest, is it? If there's a thief in this house, he won't, I don't mind saying, be found among *us*."

Desbats stood leaning against the wall, spluttering unintelligible sounds. Catherine appeared, she, too, in a nightgown, and moved close to her father. While Mathilde was explaining to her all over again that they had been waiting for Andrès to come home, and that Symphorien had been frightened, the girl, paying not the slightest attention to her mother's words, took the sick man by the shoulder and led him away.

The others heard the key turn in the lock. Gradère signed to Andrès and Mathilde to stay where they were for a moment, and to hold their breath. They could hear Catherine's voice through the wall that separated the rooms from the corridor.

"You might have caught your death! And all to no purpose.... You know I'm keeping my eyes skinned...."

"This proves that you're *not*."

"I've got to get *some* sleep, like everyone else...."

The old man mumbled something but what it was they could not hear. Catherine had gone back to bed, and she raised her voice in order to speak to him from the other room:

"*Of course not!* Really, Father, you must be out of your mind! I can believe him capable of most things, but not of that!"

Mathilde and Gradère avoided one another's eyes. She made as though to give Andrès a kiss, but he turned away his head.

There was a sound of door handles being turned, of bolts being shot. The place became once more a country house wrapped in sleep and mist a short while before cockcrow.

10.

As soon as she was dressed next morning, Mathilde knocked at her husband's door to learn his wishes before ordering the day's meals. But he did not, as he ordinarily did, call to her to come in. It was Catherine who opened the door a mere crack.

"He had a terrible time of it as a result of that fright.... He's only just got off to sleep."

"Good, then I won't wake him."

"He was fighting for breath all night, Mamma.... I thought he was dying...."

"Why didn't you come and call me?"

Catherine looked at her steadily:

"You wouldn't if you'd been me. The mere sight of you would have been enough to bring on one of his fits...."

"I've never been an object of terror to your father, my dear. He has always had complete confidence in me—what was that you said?"

Catherine uttered a harsh laugh: "Nothing," she said, and almost slammed the door shut.

Mathilde stood for a moment on the landing. She felt no anger, but, rather, that sense of relief which comes when one hears news long expected, when what one has anticipated is confirmed. She did not admit to herself that what she had heard was the cause of her present pleasure, did not even inquire whether that were, indeed, the case. "Catherine must have been exaggerating when she said she thought he was dying...those terrible coughing fits always give one that impression."

She had rested her large, handsome hands on the polished rail of the banisters. Above her head the rain was drumming on the skylight which illuminated the staircase—a steady, unbroken, settled rain. "Winter's started with a vengeance," thought Mathilde. "The Frontenac meadows will soon be lakes."

There was somebody she must see at once, somebody to whom the news she had to tell would be of great significance, unimportant though it might have seemed at first. She took a few steps along the corridor and knocked at Gabriel Gradère's door. He told her to come in; but as soon as he saw who it was seemed suddenly confused and began to make excuses:

"I didn't know it was you...I wouldn't have allowed myself..."

He was still in bed, smoking and reading a book. "Don't worry...I won't look at you..." she said with a laugh.

He buttoned up his pajama jacket, but not before she had been struck by the whiteness of his chest. Fifty years old though he was, he still had the physical attributes of a child. His body had not altered since the days when they had gone bathing in the mill pond, above the lock, and she had watched the young Gradère hesitating to dive, the drops of water sparkling on his skinny shoulders in the sun.

"Look here, Gabriel, there must be no repetition of yesterday evening's little game."

"What little game?"

She found the frankness of his gaze embarrassing. "You know perfectly well what I mean.... My husband's had a terrible night.... Catherine—though she always likes to dramatize everything so as to show me in the worst possible light—says he very nearly died..."

He crushed the stub of his cigarette into the ashtray, and she recognized as something familiar the bare arm with its undeveloped muscles, the hand covered with a rank growth of hair. His voice, when he spoke, was very quiet:

"I shouldn't have been much surprised if he had. Clairac told me that any violent emotion..."

"No!" broke in Mathilde with sudden violence. "No!"

"What do you mean—no?"

She remained silent, and, crossing to the window, pressed her forehead to the streaming pane. The world was a welter of waters. For weeks, perhaps, the rain would shroud the house and park, separating them from the outer world. They would be living, all of them, in an ark, in a ship.

Suddenly Gradère flung a question at her:

"Do you love your husband, Mathilde?"

"What a thing to ask! Of course I do!"

He smiled and lit a cigarette.

"It's difficult to explain things to you," she said. "We're not in the habit, hereabouts, of facing that sort of problem. Symphorien has remained for me, fundamentally, just precisely what he was before we got married. When my father died, he took over, as you will remember, the management of my affairs, and he has continued in the same role.... There has never been any question between us of passion or fine feelings. I am grateful to him for having piloted my ship well and truly..."

"No doubt, my dear. Still, there *was* a period when he was rather more than a mere man of business.... After all, Catherine didn't just drop from the skies..."

"Oh," she exclaimed, "all that's so long ago, and lasted for so short a while—two or three months at most. He very soon realized that it was no good his being exigent...that he wasn't intended by nature to play the part of a lover. I can swear with my hand on my heart that I find it difficult to remember, that I no longer have any clear idea of our marital relationship..."

"At heart, Mathilde, you're still a young girl...."

All of a sudden she felt that her cheeks were burning, and turned back to the window with a shrug.

"A young girl, Mathilde. You are willing to accept without repining the fact that life was over for you almost before it had begun.... But life has a way of being less cruel to us than we are to ourselves. It will not stay content with the fate we think it easier not to quarrel with, but floods back on us with a gift of just those things we thought were far removed and inaccessible...."

"I don't know what you mean," she murmured.

He continued as though he had not the slightest doubt that she would follow his meaning.

"I have a vivid recollection of the Mathilde I once knew,

of the child Mathilde, so pure and so very innocent. Still…do you remember the jouquet?"

She spoke now with passion:

"You have said enough! Don't say any more!"

Lying there on the bed, his white hair looking rough and tousled, he seemed as though sunk in a dream. A few moments passed; then, suddenly:

"Have you seen Andrès this morning?" he asked.

"No, not yet. I have nothing to say to Andrès."

"I suppose you know that his lady-love has melted into thin air? Vanished? We've got to keep him here. We've got to see that he doesn't become unmanageable. I rather hope she'll write him a letter. It's the only thing that will persuade him to be patient. Hunt for that Andrès of yours, my dear. The prospect before me is a good deal drearier. I've got to have a drink with Clairac.… The doctor and I have quite a passion for one another. I gave him a bottle of the real stuff, the sort they keep under the counter in the bars of Ciotat and Cassis… since when, he even gets up in the night for a swig.…"

Mathilde left the room with an eagerness that made her feel ashamed. "What's the matter with me?" She had a perfect right to look for Andrès, and it would be absurd to renounce it. Besides, she must keep an eye on him. She knew him only too well. He would never stand up to pain. She felt feverish—worked on, at one and the same time, by apprehension and hope.

She entered his room as usual, without knocking. He was standing in front of the mirror, bare-armed, engaged in shaving himself. He turned on her in a blazing temper:

"This isn't a millhouse! Have I got to lock my door?"

She stood on the threshold, overcome by the nature of her reception:

"But Andrès, darling...I suppose I *do* treat you like a little boy...."

She could have thought of nothing better calculated to calm him. He walked across the room and kissed her:

"You're just dear old Tamati...."

He gave her another kiss but she did not return it, but left the room. He followed her into the corridor.

"Postman not come yet?"

"Of course not, dear. You know he never turns up till between eleven and twelve."

From now on he would live for the postman, she thought. One can give one's mind only to a single person at a time. One person, and one only, exists for us: we can do no more than make pretend that we believe in the reality of any others. His "old Tamati"—she shook her head, as though she were chasing away a wasp, and went into the kitchen to give the day's orders to Gercinthe. On her way upstairs later, she ran into Catherine.

"I was looking for you, Mamma.... Father wants to see you.... There's no need to run," she added in an edged voice.

By the time she reached her husband's room, Mathilde was noticeably out of breath. He was sitting as usual, huddled in his chair. She could not remember when she had seen him last in bed. He was unshaven and unwashed. She felt as though his brooding eyes were reading deep in her mind. She could hear the whistling sound made by his breathing. He was smoking an herbal cigarette. "Sit closer, so I needn't strain myself.... I'm no worse in myself, but I'm getting more and more breathless. When it comes on in the autumn it's always worse and lasts longer.... I want to have a chat with you, to ask you a question.... Look here, Mathilde, in spite of what happened last night, I trust you.... But I'd like to be sure you aren't in a plot with the others against me, that you're still a free agent. Promise me that is so and I'll believe you. I want to believe you. Catherine's only a child, I can't talk to her; besides, she takes things too hard."

It was true. There was probably only one person in the world of whom Symphorien Desbats was not suspicious, and that one person was his wife. She was as well aware of that as of the prestige she enjoyed in his sight. But she did not know the underlying reason for his attitude. *She* might pretend that she had almost forgotten the two or three months of her married life of which she had been reminded while talking to Gradère, but to him they were an ever-present reality. Her old husband remembered only too well his wretched moments of failure, his no less wretched moments of success, and he was grateful to Mathilde for never having held them against him, for having always been attentive to his wishes, for having unfailingly given him good advice, except where Andrès' interests were in question.

She answered him, now, carefully weighing her words. "There is no plot. If one existed, and I knew of it, I should have told you. But don't be in a hurry to thank me. I'm only too conscious of what you've been hatching against Andrès."

"You're wrong, my dear...I swear it.... I knew, of course, that Catherine had her knife into him, but up to the last moment I thought she would agree to marry him, because, as no one knows better than you, she's a mad creature."

Seeing that Mathilde looked surprised, he developed what was in his mind:

"I mean it: if she weren't, she would never have resented his indifference. Time and time again she has said to me—'If only he'd try to deceive me, if only he'd pretend....' She knew all about this love affair of his long before the rest of you...so, you see, I had some reason for believing that she would agree to marry him in the end, no matter how often she told me she wouldn't...and I rather dreaded it. I know how fond you are of him, my dear. But just think what Andrès *is*, what it would have meant to have him as a son-in-law. He's not a bad lad, but he *is* the child of..."

The sick man glanced uneasily at the door and lowered his voice:

"You don't know what I know. You've no idea what Gradère's capable of, of what may burst on us at any moment—I have my spies—and when the worst happens, you'll thank me on your bended knees for having done what I could to prevent that awful man from becoming your daughter's father-in-law. If such a day should ever dawn, it would be a day of shame for us." He was drawing his breath now so painfully, and speaking in a tone of such fervor, that Mathilde was frightened. "Why, the police might come for him in this very house.... Of course, he's only our cousin by marriage, but Andrès being there makes him one of the family...I can't talk to you openly...Catherine's the only person to whom..."

Mathilde drew her chair closer.

"You can trust me," she murmured. "You know I'm as silent as the tomb. I don't *want* Andrès to marry Catherine."

It was the first time she had shown any sign that she was

opposed to the marriage. She had always behaved as though Andrès' happiness depended on it. The sick man pressed his wife's hand with an expression on his face of trust and joy. He could tell her everything!

"If you need proof of how much she wants him, you need only realize what a good offer she's refused…Berbiney's boy…Berbiney, my partner at the factory.…In spite of the drop in real property values, their land is still worth an awful lot…and land will go up again once they've re-valued the franc—as they're bound to do. My poor dear, the fact that we've never discussed all this before shows how far apart we've drifted during the last two or three years!"

"It stands to reason"—she broke in vehemently—"that you couldn't talk about this Berbiney scheme while you were making me believe all the time that you wanted to give Catherine to Andrès! Now that you've stripped him of Cernes and Balisaou…"

"But just consider for a moment. His father would have made him sell them, in any case. You must know perfectly well that he leads Andrès by the nose. What matters is that Cernes and Balisaou should not be allowed to go out of the family. You do agree about that, don't you? Why, the thing's self-obvious. If they did, there would be a bit of somebody else's land jutting into the estate, and that would make it impossible for the property to be held as a single whole. I did no more than my duty," he added with a disarming air of conviction. "I've told you the bare, unvarnished truth. Up to the very last minute I was afraid the girl might fling herself into his arms. As to the wretched Andrès, *he's* been fleeced by his swine of a father even before the money's been paid over.

As it is, I'm indemnifying him. Until I die he'll live rent-free, with an allowance considerably in excess of anything Cernes and Balisaou would have brought him—and they'll still be in the family. When I'm gone, and if you survive me—because one never knows who's going to live and who's going to die—well, you can give him just as much as you like—but in cash, mind—you're not to make over a single foot of land to him. You must swear that you won't do that! But how do we know where Andrès will be when that time comes? I'm really very sorry for him. He's not a bad lad, but, well, that's how things are—the children pay for the sins of their fathers—it's a law of nature."

Mathilde was listening to him with deep attention. She had recovered her self-control, and was now perfectly cool and collected. The important thing for her was to find out the precise nature of the threat hanging over Gabriel's head, so that she might be able to put him on his guard. She would not accept the "law of nature" of which her husband had spoken. It was a wicked law, and she was determined that it should not apply in Andrès' case. But Gradère, so she told herself, could stand up to the whole world. He only needed to be warned. He would find some way of countering the attack that had been planned at his expense.

"I am very glad that we have had this talk, Symphorien. I can't agree that you have treated Andrès properly, but I do believe now that you acted in good faith."

He took his wife's hand and pressed it.

"You *must* trust me. You know how fond I am of Andrès.… It is essential that I know the nature of the danger that is hanging over his father…so that I can get his son out of harm's way...protect him...send him off somewhere in good time.... It might, for instance, be possible for him to go on a trip to Norway.... He ought to have a look at the paper mills.... Come closer and listen to me" (the old man lowered his voice to a whisper). "I've known for some time that a woman is blackmailing Gradère—he told me so himself, though it wouldn't have been difficult to guess. Now, if a resourceful fellow like that lets himself be sucked dry, year after year, it can only mean that *she's* in possession of a pretty deadly weapon.... I've discovered the address of this Aline creature—it wasn't hard, I only had to take a peep at Gradère's mail last time he was here. He's a man of great determination. Nothing will get him out of this house. He's made up his mind to do me down. He's strong, and I, Mathilde, feel very weak when I'm up against him...because of my state of health.... Clairac thinks I'm worse. He never says it in so many words, but...and I'd never tell this to anyone but you... he's becoming a bit of an alarmist. I don't really believe in all his gloomy talk, because I'm pretty sure I'm not near so bad as he makes out...but, well, the sooner we can get rid of that swine Gradère, the better—don't you agree?—no matter what it costs.... I wrote a letter to this woman Aline, and the answer came this morning. What it amounts to is that she agrees to take him off our hands. She'll turn up here when he least expects it. It'll cost me a pretty penny, but I shan't pay her until she's proved as good as her word. This time she's quite resolved to sink him because she knows he's at the end of his resources. I've offered her what amounts to a small fortune on condition that she does the job thoroughly. You know whom I mean by the Marquis de Dorth? I told you all about his wife's letters which Gradère was showing round before disposing of them to her husband for a hundred thousand francs…the daughter was engaged to a man who's since backed out as a result of the scandal.… I hear she's gone completely out of her mind.… But that's no business of ours. The only thing that matters to *us* is that the Marquis means to have his scalp, that he's said what he's willing to pay, and that this Aline creature has struck a bargain. If Gradère looks like being arrested, or even cornered, if it comes to that, I think you'll agree it's best that the business should come to a head as far from here as possible, though once the mud's been stirred up, we're bound to be splattered no matter how far off we are."

Mathilde wanted to cry out "We must stop it! For Andrès' sake we must stop it!" but restrained herself. Nothing now would alter her husband's determination. She must pursue the plan she had already thought out—pretend to fall in with the old man's wishes, discover as much as she could, and then warn Gabriel. Because of Andrès she must take sides with the villain of the piece, for the man *was* a villain, even if, only a short while ago, he had been able to set her trembling merely by uttering the word—"jouquet." Thirty years ago she had laid her head, in all innocence, on his bony shoulder, and closed her eyes. She could still remember the noise made by the curtain of the falling rain. It had been the one and only adventure of her life. Everything that mattered to her had been contained within the walls of a "jouquet." Life had brought her nothing else, and now nothing else would ever be hers.… Nothing? Preyed upon though she was by the confused medley of her thoughts, she was still all ears for what the old man was about to tell her.

"The letters I write her are quite impersonal, and, naturally, I don't sign them with my name. I'm nothing if not cautious! There is no indication at all to show where they come from. So she shan't guess anything from the envelopes, I always give them to Berbiney when he goes into Bordeaux on Mondays. I send nothing from Liogeats—don't trust the postmistress. Well, to cut a long story short, this precious Aline's due to arrive on Monday evening—in three days' time. Catherine will meet her at the station. As soon as she gets here, we'll let her loose in Gradère's bedroom. She'll catch him fast asleep. 'I guarantee,' she wrote me, 'that he'll leave with me by the first train on Tuesday.' Things are beginning to hum, as Andrès would say.... Oh, yes, they'll hum all right. I'm doing the boy a service, you know" (with a nervous glance at Mathilde). "Once the blow has fallen, he'll forget the whole business in next to no time, and we can keep him with us here. What's the point of sending him on his travels, and spending a lot of money? He'll go on looking after the estate just as though it were his own, and, in the long run, Catherine will make a match of it with the Berbiney boy.... You're not going?"

"Of course not," said Mathilde, who had got up. "But I think you're talking too much and getting too excited."

She made as though to put her hand on his forehead, but he seized it and pressed it to his dry lips.

"Catherine would be furious if she knew I'd been confiding in you. She's not fair where you're concerned...jealous, I suppose. But I don't regret anything. On the contrary, I feel distinctly reassured.... You've always had a horror of the fellow and you've every reason to hate him, if only on Adila's account."

In a voice that seemed to sound the very note of frankness, she replied:

"I don't know whether I hate him, but I certainly think him horrible.... He frightens me, too—there's no doubt about that!"

The sick man, freed of his anxiety, rubbed his hands with an air of jubilation, till the joints cracked.

"My mind's at rest now. All you've got to do is to keep Andrès' attention occupied. Once we're through, I'm sure you can convince him that what has happened is all for the best."

Only just in time she snatched away her hand which he had been pressing between his own. Catherine came into the room and shot a suspicious look at the pair of them. Mathilde found relief in the joy of having something to tell, the same sort of joy as sets children running when the excitement of impending disaster has hold of them. But it would be rash to go straight to Gradère, because Catherine, no doubt, would keep a watchful eye on both of them.... She understood, now, the reason for the doctor's alarmist words to his patient. Gabriel was strong—stronger than any of them, and he would find some way of parrying the blow.

It was raining harder than ever. Mathilde remained on the watch in her room, holding the window slightly parted so as to be able to make a sign to Gradère when he came back. She felt far from bored as she waited. To have occupied the time in any other way would have been beyond her power. She, too, was driving straight to her goal, to that vast, vague happiness towards which she had been moving ever since Gabriel's return. She would reach it at last, thanks to him, for he was powerful enough to open its gates to her.... What harm was she doing? Why should she feel ill at ease? If she had had to make her confession at that very moment, there was no crime of which she could have accused herself. Was it not her duty to warn Gradère? His life was at stake, Adila's husband's life, Andrès' father's. "But," said a secret voice within her, "you know perfectly well that Gradère means nothing to you. You know perfectly well what to expect of him...."

"I expect nothing!" she said aloud.

SHE was seated with Andrès and Catherine at the table when Gradère entered. Mealtimes now had become occasions of silence. Catherine got up before the sweet course, and left the room to go to her father. Mathilde took advantage of the brief respite, when she heard the girl's footsteps overhead and knew that she was not being spied upon, to murmur to Gradère that there was something very important she had to tell him, and that he must meet her in a safe place. But nowhere in the daytime was safe, because the rain kept everyone indoors.

"Come to my room tonight," said Gradère. "It's the furthest from the old man's."

"But suppose I was caught—what would people think?"

"You won't be caught, and besides, we've got other things to worry about. What you want to tell me is pretty serious. I've a pretty shrewd idea what it is.... It's about Aline, isn't it?"

She nodded assent. He raised his two fists and let them fall.

"Ah! That woman!"

At sight of the hatred in his face, Mathilde turned away her eyes.

11.

Late the same afternoon, Andrès was lying on his bed smoking the last cigarette from the packet he had opened that morning. He had spread a newspaper under his feet so that his muddy boots should not dirty the coverlet.

Through the door came the voice of Gercinthe saying that the curé would like a word with him.

"It's you he's asking for, Monsieur Andrès.... I've shown him into the big drawing room."

It was only after the lapse of some seconds that Andrès' mind established a connection between "the curé" and "Tota's brother." In a flash he was off the bed. This was the long-awaited answer, Tota's answer, given in about as bad a form as it well could be. Now that the wretched curé was mixed up in the business, there was no hope left. He ran down the stairs without even bothering to smooth his hair, and burst, a tousled figure with drawn face and open collar, into the huge, gloomy room which, in spite of the radiators, was icy cold. Armchairs covered in dust-sheets stood against the wall, flanked by large consoles in fake buhl. Above them hung a row of fairly good portraits, by the early nineteenth-century Bordeaux painter, Gallard, of members of the Du Buch family. The crystal chandelier, enveloped in a muslin bag, was reflected in the shiny surface of a heavy Empire table on which lay photograph albums, a draught-board, and a stereoscopic apparatus, in the middle of all this litter was the curé's hat, an odd, battered object, looking like a dead bat. Andrès gave a sidelong glance at the little priest whose squat, thickset figure was not unlike his own (there was some excuse for the mistake made by Mouleyre and Pardieu). But in the young man's serious and prematurely lined face he could read neither shame nor anguish. For Andrès the word "priest" stood for a jumble of ready-made ideas about which he had never taken the trouble to think. He had been one of those innumerable children who "make their Communion" because it is the customary thing to do, who never concern themselves with its implications. Had he been pressed to give his views, it would have been obvious that he looked on the whole business as boring and unimportant, as something of which it would be time enough to talk when he was lying at death's door, as something that gives a gloss of respectability to weddings and funerals. The only other feeling of which he was conscious, as he looked at this young and lonely celibate, was one of profound masculine disgust and physical loathing.

"I think, sir," began the priest, "that you must have guessed on whose behalf I have come to see you?"

Andrès made no movement, but stood with his head bent slightly forward as though he were awaiting a blow on the back of the neck.

The other continued: "I have some knowledge of what you feel for somebody who is very dear to me…. You must be brave. She has done what I had given up hoping she would do, something that ought to make you as happy as it makes me—because I do you the credit of believing that your love is genuine. She has gone back to her husband. I had a line from her this morning to that effect."

"So you've got your way, after all!" broke in Andrès, and there was a note of bitter hatred in his voice.

The Abbé stammered in reply that the news of this decision had come as a great surprise to him, that he had long given up any hope of it, that he still felt bewildered.

"People are right when they talk about the power of the priests," said Andrès. "You always manage to get your way."

"You are wrong: I am very far from having any power."

Unused though he was to observing his fellows, Andrès was struck by the tone of voice in which this was said, and, raising his eyes, looked straight at Tota's brother. The realization that he *was* her brother prompted the stare that he directed at him. There was nothing in the man's features to remind him of the woman, yet there was, as it were, an echo of her in the lined and hollow cheeks, in the bend of the mouth, in the way the nose was set, in the quality of the look that returned his own…an echo of all that he had lost.

Words suddenly burst from him: "You can't possibly know…I'm not blaming you…you can't possibly know…."

The Abbé took him shyly by the hand. Andrès made to attempt to withdraw it.

"You priests," went on the young man, "don't understand these things. You don't realize what love means."

He was amazed to hear a low laugh which the other quickly suppressed. He looked at the priest, who said quite simply:

"Do you really believe that?"

The little spurt of laughter came again. Suddenly, in the impersonal tones of a confessor addressing his penitent, the Abbé went on:

"You love greatly, but you must love more greatly still—by renouncing her."

Andrès was moved once more to furious rebellion: "You don't know what you're talking about! Do you think my renunciation is going to make her happy? You regard me as a fool, like the rest of them. But just you wait! I'll find some way of getting to her!"

"That would not be particularly difficult...a poor, hunted creature.... But my object in coming here" (there was a change in his voice, he was not far from tears) "was to beg you—for I know you have a good heart and have always sided with the poor—to have pity on her. I don't intend to talk about myself. You can't know—you are young—but because you are young you should be able to understand what a life like mine is like...quite probably Tota has discussed it with you. I am the same age as you—twenty-six. Everyone either hates or despises me. Even my superiors think me guilty of imprudence. The thought of her is the only thing that keeps me going.... I have never said as much to anyone before...you are the first. I implore you in the name of that God who will one day show Himself in His strength, which is greater than the strength of our mad desire to achieve damnation...."

Life is rich in such extraordinary instances of the dispro-
portion between the one who confides and the one who
receives the confidence. The explanation is that the choice is
taken out of our hands. A moment comes when agony must
find an outlet, must tear itself free of the suffering womb.
And when that happens, any arms will do, any arms at all,
to take in custody the dark child of the soul. If Andrès in his
youth and his simplicity did not fully understand the meaning of the words that he heard, he could, nevertheless, feel the
torment that informed them.

He said:

"I'm not forgetting that I owe Mouleyre and Pardie a
good punch on the jaw, and they'll get it, too. From now on,
people are going to leave you alone—you can take my word
for that."

Much later, Alain was to remember this moment, and
how, suddenly, he had known with certainty that this youth
who looked so strong, so self-sufficient, was already eddying
like a straw in the wind. He had realized then that his presence in this room was not due to mere chance. The thought
of Tota ceased to occupy his mind. She had no part to play
any longer in the misery that gripped his heart. To himself
he said: "Have mercy, Lord, upon those who dwell in this
house!"

Andrès, seeing that the other's eyes were brimming with
tears, felt quite overwhelmed. In response to one of those
generous impulses that come to the very young, he gripped
his hand:

"I make no promise," he said, uncertainly. "I want her too
badly. But I'll fight as long as I can."

The Abbé nodded. He was beyond the power of speech, and looked long and intently at the boy.

Andrès opened the door. In the dark hallway a man was smoking, a man still young in spite of his silver hair, wearing a shooting coat. A handkerchief of the same color as his shirt projected from his pocket. The smell of his cigarette reminded the Abbé of Tota's room.

"I don't know whether you know my father, sir." Gradère got up from his chair. Although the rainy dusk made it impossible to see any of the faces clearly, the priest felt himself transfixed by the gaze of this man about whom people said so much that was bad. He had responded to the introduction with a low bow. Then he hurried on, shut the front door behind him rather too sharply, and disappeared into the dusk and the rain.

He had gone only a few paces, struggling against the damp wind which set his soutane billowing, when he heard the sound of somebody running after him. He turned. It was the man, Andrès' father, bare-headed, his hair blowing wildly.

"I'd like to have a word with you...."

Alain, who was considerably the shorter, had to raise his face in order to hear. The sense of antipathy, of repulsion with which this almost invisible stranger filled him, made him feel ashamed. How he hated those gentle, almost honeyed tones!

"I have written you a letter, sir—though perhaps letter is hardly the right word.... I should say, rather, a volume, containing the story of my life, my very terrible life. But I broke off in the middle.... I lacked the courage. But now I know that I had to write it, that you have to read it.... May

I leave this notebook with you? Just a plain, school exercise book. You can answer it or not, as you think best."

Alain made a sign of assent. "I am at the call of any man," he replied with a trace of affectation. But he did not take the other's hand.

Gradère went back to the house, feeling chilled to the bone. Andrès had not noticed his absence.

"Papa, he came to ask me…he came because of his sister." Misery choked him, so that he had to break off. "You'll tell me that I've only got to make up my mind…that all I need to do is hunt her out…"

His father, whose face he could not see, interrupted the flow of words:

"No, my boy, I shan't tell you that."

Andrès thought, "He's afraid I'm going to ask him for money so I can join her in Paris."

But Gradère's words bore quite a different sense:

"You can trust that little priest, I feel sure of that."

The young man showed no sign of surprise.

"Nothing matters to me any longer, Papa," he said, and his voice was eloquent of weariness and despair. "My marriage has come to nothing—well, I don't care. As to Cernes and Balisaou—you've got the money…and I don't give a fig for anything else. What point is there in my staying on here? What possible point?" He broke off but continued a moment later in a lower voice: "I didn't much like that talk we had yesterday evening—though I expect you'll think me a fool for saying so…. Why all this plotting? There's nothing more to keep you at Liogeats." By this time it was pitch dark. Andrès might well have thought that his father had vanished. He could not even catch the sound of his breathing. But suddenly he heard his voice raised in the darkness. There was an edge to it that was unusual:

"You're wrong, my boy…there's something still to be done here.… As soon as my task is finished, I promise you I'll go and you shall never see me again."

Andrès could think of nothing to say. He was not used to reading his own moods, to observing his own reactions. He belonged to that innumerable race of young people who find it enough to say "I've got a fit of the blues!"—finding in that word a sufficient explanation of all the myriad source of their misery and despair.

Suddenly, in the silence, he heard the sound of the door being quietly closed, and realized that his father was no longer with him.

12.

"I'll wait a bit before leaving your room," said Gradère in a low voice. "Your talk with the old man must have roused Catherine's suspicions. She's very much on the alert. If she saw me go out…"

Mathilde replied: "Stay a little longer, then."

They could hear, outside the house, a quiet, all-enveloping rustle of rain, broken at irregular intervals by the sharp sound of drops falling from the roof on to the balcony. The bedside lamp gave only a dim light. Mathilde could just make out a man's shadowy bulk on the sofa. His elbows were on his knees and he was biting his nails.

He knew the whole truth now. She had told him everything and already bitterly repented having done so. She was terrified by the sense of controlled power that he gave her. He had shown neither surprise nor anger, had uttered no exclamation. But had he given free rein to his fury Mathilde would have found it infinitely preferable to his present attitude. The close attention with which he had followed her every word, the calm way in which he had questioned her about the details of the scheme, had impressed her more unpleasantly than any outburst could have done. And now, here he was, harking back to the same points:

"You're quite sure it's Catherine who is to meet her at the station? You're clear that Desbats told you he had typed the letters on unheaded paper, and had them posted in Bordeaux? That's very important."

"Why is it important?" she asked.

He made an evasive gesture and plunged once more into his silent thoughts. She looked across the room at him. His hands were clasped tightly, and he was holding them against his cheek. It was she who had set this invincible machine in motion. She was like a careless child who throws away a match. Suddenly the forest is a mass of flame. The tocsin sounds from steeple to steeple, and the roads are a hurly-burly of cars and carts.... In vain she had begged Gradère to go away, to find some hiding place. He had chosen instead to face the coming danger. She ought never to have spoken. Aline, in that case, would have come and would have taken him away with her.... There would have been a brief scandal, a stirring of the waters...and then, a blanketing silence. They would have sent Andrès to Scandinavia.... She had always been against that trip, but now would welcome it.... Useless to think of these things. The die was cast, unless...she *could* throw herself at Symphorien's feet and admit her treachery. A telegram *could* be sent telling Aline to postpone her journey. Tragedy *could* be averted.... Such were her thoughts as she walked up and down the room.

It was Gradère now who followed her with his eyes, watching her closely. He was aware of the danger. He had always had these sudden intuitions which revealed to him what his adversary was thinking. He could smell treason even before it had taken shape in the mind of his accomplice. He asked:

"You're sure Catherine's not going to take the car so as to avoid attracting attention—sure that they're going to walk back from the station?"

"Since you seem to know the answer, why ask me?"

"Oh, well, let's change the subject. I, too, have got a piece of news for you. The Abbé Forcas came to see Andrès this afternoon. I suppose you can guess why? It seems that the lady has made it up with her husband. The little priest did a bit of coaxing, and our Andrès has given up all ideas, for the time being, at least, of pressing his advantage...."

Mathilde uttered an "Ah!" and paused in her pacing to and fro.

"It's a matter of great importance for us, for you. It means that you'll have to take him on, watch him—though without seeming to—surround him with attentions.... But don't go on treating him as though he were a child. Change your methods. What he needs now is the presence in his life of a woman, of a woman's tenderness. Things may start moving pretty quickly now, believe me! But whatever you do, don't worry. I have a perfect right to take steps for my own protection. Whatever happens, don't forget that my first duty is to save my own skin."

He came close to her:

"You'll be free very soon now, Mathilde."

"But I don't need to be free," she exclaimed with vehemence. "There's nothing I want...nothing, I tell you."

Gradère signed to her to speak more quietly. Going to the door he pressed his ear to it.

"I think I can get back to my room now.... I quite understand, my dear, that you want nothing that you haven't got already. But *suppose* things should happen to you...the kind of things you're not counting on and never think about, what then? Oh, well, wait and see. I'm not worrying. You haven't committed a single mistake since the game started. I shall never forget the service you've done me this evening. And you won't forget, either, in the days now very close at hand, when even at night you will no longer be separated from Andrès, that you owe your happiness to me...."

She stifled a cry: "Stop! You...you...filthy beast!"

But he was no longer there.

It did not occur to her to undress. She just stood in the middle of the room, thinking of nothing. She seemed to draw a positive happiness from this complete vacuity of mind. The idea came to her that she would take a soporific, so as to get to sleep more quickly. The medicine-cupboard was in her dressing room which had a frosted and shutterless window looking out on the stable yard.

"Better," she thought, "not to switch on the light," and started to fumble among the various tubes and bottles, trying to find what she was looking for. Bergère began to bark, then stopped. What was that creaking? She recognized the sound: it was made by the wooden door of the tool-shed. She climbed onto a stool and pushed the window slightly open. It was no longer raining, but the whole forest was dripping. Each time the wind rose it was as though another shower had started. It was not cold. Mathilde sniffed with delight the smell of rain-drenched earth. She had not been mistaken. Someone was coming from the tool-shed carrying a spade on his shoulder. He was making no attempt to conceal his movements. He seemed to know that none of the bedrooms looked out onto the yard. He must, therefore, be someone familiar with the house. As a matter of fact, she had already recognized in him the man who, a quarter of an hour before, had been sitting with her in her room. Perhaps he had gone mad! He must be mad, for he had no business out of doors at that hour of the night, whether for good purposes or bad. "He had the look of a madman, had spoken like a madman," thought Mathilde as she went back to her room and swallowed two tablets. She preferred to think of him as that, to persuade herself that her diagnosis was correct. In any case, what she had caught him doing constituted no threat to anyone. Symphorien was fast asleep only a few yards away, and Aline had not yet left Paris. It would be time to begin worrying when Monday came.

Sleep was longer delayed than she had expected, but her limbs felt languid, her body comfortably relaxed. She remembered suddenly that she had forgotten to say her prayers. That would mean having to get up again and kneel down. Her courage failed her, and she compromised by hastily murmuring a few set phrases without in the least taking in what she was saying. Her fine arms closed about the ghost of an absent form. She felt upon her body a vast presence, light as a feather.

13.

ON Monday morning Gercinthe called through the door, in her usual way:

"Mademoiselle Catherine wanted on the telephone."

Seeing that the girl showed signs of surprise, her father said:

"Must be the factory."

Apprehension of the coming explosion had increased his breathlessness. "That woman" would be with them by evening, and he would take her straight to Gradère's room. Would blessed release come to them with the morrow? Gradère had great reserves of strength, but not where Aline was concerned. She had kept a tight hold on him for twenty years, and he had never been able to make her loosen her grasp. Could it be that Mathilde had been guilty of treachery? No, he had no anxiety on that score. Catherine had been watching her carefully, and was sure that nothing had passed between her and Gradère. She might, of course, have slipped a note to him, but the girl would have got wind of it. Here she was, back again.

"It was a call from Paris, Papa…that woman, Aline. She won't be here till Thursday…. She's had the flu, but not badly. She says she'll arrive on Thursday without fail."

"Did you speak to her personally?"

"Yes, *what* a voice…thick and husky…I've never heard one like it!"

"Well, we must wait till Thursday…though I regret the delay. In matters of this sort, speed's the great thing."

Catherine was busy with her thoughts:

"Two more days. By that time it may have stopped raining, and the walk from the station won't be so awful. I don't fancy floundering along a flooded road with that monster! I suppose you warned her it was a good twenty minutes' tramp?"

"Certainly I did, and it's the item of the program she finds least to her taste. But she realizes how necessary it is to take precautions with a chap as dangerous as that. The slut ought to know him if anyone does!"

"I've made a discovery, Papa. Now don't get worked up. It's not important, and the main thing is that we should be warned in time. For the last few days Clairac's been taking his apéritif at Lacote's with…"

"Not Gradère?"

Catherine nodded.

"Are you quite sure?"

"But what does it matter, Papa? You can always show Clairac the door, and have Pétiot instead…he's just as good a doctor."

"Maybe, but he doesn't know my constitution," groaned the invalid. "Besides, it's very significant. It shows, don't you see, how Gradère is trimming his sails. It's positively terrifying. I feel nervous on your account, too. He wants to get you out of the way. He'll hit on something, though I don't know what. Poison, perhaps...."

Catherine murmured:

"He's welcome to kill me if he wants to!"

But the old man did not hear her, and went on:

"That's why Clairac's been trying to frighten me lately. It was that fellow's doing. He wants to work on my nerves. Well, it's better I should know...and there's life in the old dog yet... Still, that doesn't alter the fact that we *do* live too much cut off here.... Ah, dear child, if only" (a wheedling tone crept into his voice) "if only you could bring yourself to say yes... young Berbiney..."

She interrupted him almost aggressively: "You've forgotten the terms of our agreement: not another word on the subject until the first of January...."

"But when I made that promise, I didn't know the sort of threat we should have to face. Just think what it would mean to have a man about the house, a big sturdy young fellow of no more than thirty on our side...a chap who could take that swine by the back of the neck and chuck him out of the window."

"But don't forget, Papa, that Gradère is in his son's house here, which is as much as to say, in his own. Why shouldn't we move? Your old house on the Square is still empty...."

"What? Leave the chateau? Never!"

All his life he had dreamt of being the undisputed master of the chateau of Liogeats. But so long as Andrès had been a minor, it had been impossible for him to set aside the legal act which enforced their holding of the house in joint ownership, and, for the last year, the young man, egged on by his father and Mathilde, had resolutely refused to sell his share.

"To think that I am part-owner with the son of *that* horror.... As for your precious Andrès, I confess that I'm getting heartily sick of the sight of his little bullet-head."

"You can say what you like about him, but no one can accuse him of being ugly."

"He seems handsome to you, because you've never seen other boys."

It was true enough; she never *had* seen other boys, though she had more than once been present at weddings, and went regularly to the races at Lugdunos and Bazas. There had been young men and to spare at those festivities, but with what eyes had she looked at them? For her there was but one young man in the world, and she might, had she so wished, have been his wife, ignored perhaps, even detested, but still his wife. At times he would have had to take her in his arms if only to be sure of having a family. What she occasionally imagined, or, rather, what she forbade herself to imagine (it was the sole burden of her confessions) would then have been a duty and not a sin. It wouldn't matter that he did not love her.

"What are you thinking about, my dear?"

"I was listening to the rain and thinking how nice it is that I needn't go and meet that woman tonight."

About four o'clock on that same Monday, Catherine heard the car. She went to the window and saw Gradère enter the house and then leave it again almost immediately.

"Gradère's going out," she said. "He's carrying something, but, I can't quite see what it is. Where can he be off to so late? It's not time for the postman yet."

"Quick! Go after him, my dear. Today of all days, we must neglect nothing."

Catherine took down her oilskin and opened the door, as only she knew how, so that it made no sound. Symphorien heard her running down the path. To while away the time till her return, he took one of the ledgers from the pile that stood on the small table, within reach of his hand, and began to check the columns of figures.

She came back sooner than he had expected.

"Well?"

"You'll never guess! He went to the curé's house with a great fat envelope. Nobody answered his knock, and he pushed it under the door. Then he came home. Had you realized that he knew the Abbé Forcas?"

Sympholien pondered:

"I've no idea what they can have in common except this affair of Andrès with his sister."

"Of course!" said Catherine angrily. "The letter must have had something to do with that squalid business!"

14.

ON that particular Monday, the curé had been out on his bicycle, visiting some of the outlying farms (he was more likely to get a friendly welcome there than in the town). He got back about six o'clock, worn out but happy in the knowledge that he had been kindly entertained in four or five of the houses at which he had called. He had been invited to drink with his hosts, had given their children sacred pictures, and had taken the names of several boys for his confirmation classes. On his way home through Liogeats, Madame Larose, who kept the draper's shop, had asked him at what time he would be saying Mass on the first Friday in December. To crown all, a group of workmen belonging to the Desbats-Berbiney factory, had raised their caps to him. It needed no more than that to restore his self-confidence. Fortune had been smiling on him ever since Tota had gone back to her husband. He had picked up Gradère's envelope as he entered the house. He knew from whom it came, and the sight of it again brought on his gloomy mood. He felt tempted to throw it unopened into a drawer. But after a hurried meal, he went upstairs to his bedroom, put on his slippers…and was soon deep in the contents of the thin exercise book.

An oil lamp stood on the small table beside his pillow, lighting from below the hanging crucifix. He completed a page, paused for breath, raised his eyes to the figure of Christ as though to draw strength from it, and plunged once more into the sea of mud with feelings not so much of horror as of fear. The mystery of evil, brooding on which had always been his besetting temptation, that mystery at the thought of which Tota's brother had more than once lost heart, was here in his hands, packed tight between the blue covers of a small, ruled exercise book. He read without pausing until he reached the passage where Gradère, obsessed by the Devil, had quoted something said to him by an old priest: "there are human souls that have been given to *him*."

"No!" he protested in aloud voice: "No, oh God, not that!" Alain did not believe that any soul could be given over entirely to "him," for, if that were so, then all souls must be in like predicament, because, ever since the Fall, each generation of men had inherited from their forebears enough of evil to ensure their damnation—an obscure madness which, starting far back in the history of the Race, had been embodied in every individual, down to those still living—vices kept in chains by some, triumphant in others, coming to rank flower in great-great-nephews.

But had not an invisible being been given power over this corrupt substance, to hammer it into dust—an archangel? (Though most men did not even know of his existence.) Not only does he pound the hideous refuse of their poor hearts.

He can make use of the longing in them for tenderness, of the passionate desire they feel to give themselves....

"Lord," thought Alain, "I, too, know what loneliness means. And You, too, know well, having suffered it unto death in the night of that fatal Thursday and Friday, what loneliness a man may feel when the Father has abandoned him... do not permit your Enemy, the Power of Darkness, the Prince of this World, to use it for his purpose of damnation.... But whence comes his power? To whom is he answerable for his Princedom?"

From the little exercise book with its innocent blue covers streamed an unending host of prostitutes and pimps, of homosexuals and drug addicts and murderers. Brothels and prisons and penitentiaries, all the restrictive institutions of the State, showed to the eyes of his spirit as a sort of subterranean hive, as an invisible crypt, beneath the visible city. At this very moment, on a desert track in Africa, a penal battalion was marching to the tune of a filthy song.... Alain knew that he was prey to temptation, to his own peculiar temptation. Not the kingdoms of this earth were spread beneath his eyes, but its shameful secrets.

He had fallen to his knees, his hands clasped on the open exercise book. Those hands of his, formed to bless and to absolve, were in contact with the page where, beneath each line, was the faint mark left by Gradère's fingernail. This ordained priest was praying on a written record of crime. In an effort of obedience he reminded himself of what had been taught him at the Seminary. No human creature has anything in himself but lies and sin. The power to love God is in the gift of God alone, and His love is His recompense to us for what His love has given. But if it is He who is the source of all good, it is we who are the source of all evil.

Each time that we perform some act of goodness, it is God who operates in us and through us; but every act of evil belongs to us, and to us alone. Where evil is concerned, we are, to some extent, as gods.

"This man, Gradère, has chosen to be a god?"

But all these truths that Alain strove to remember fell on the anguish of his soul like snow on a fire. Snow! Snow! He was reminded that a holy woman had once seen the souls of the damned falling into darkness like innumerable snow-flakes. Not all the rustling of the rain upon the presbytery roof and the flooded roads could break the almost tangible silence of that living snow, of those layers on layers of human souls falling, falling, piling up on one another in an endless descent. He made a violent effort to resist—even before it had taken shape—a criminal desire to be himself a flake among those other flakes, a temptation (which filled him with horror) not to separate himself from the great host of the damned. He emptied his mind of all thought, made in himself a void, forced himself to be a spirit waiting…waiting. And from the depths of the ages came to his ears, distinct, the answer that Christ had made to that Apostle who had asked: "Who then can be saved?" "With men this is impossible; but with God all things are possible."

With love all things are possible. Love turns the logic of the Doctors to foolishness. Did the wretched man who had poured into this child's exercise book all the abomination of his life know of what good he was capable? Those who seem dedicated to evil may, perhaps, be chosen above their fellows:

the very depth of their fall gives a measure of the vocation that they have betrayed. None would be blessed had they not been given the power to damn themselves. Perhaps, only those are damned who might have been saints.

Thus did Alain meditate upon his knees, his hands clasped upon a schoolboy's exercise book. The rain fell harder. He told himself that it was rustling with just the same sound on the roof of the chateau of Liogeats, where, in one of the rooms, the poor soul who had covered these pages with scrawled writing was lying fast asleep. He was the father of that Andrès whom Tota had loved.... At that moment, he had an almost physical sense of the co-inherence of human souls, of that mysterious union in which we are all of us involved alike by sin and grace. He wept for very love of sinners. The whistle of a train came to his ears through the darkness. The wheels of a long line of trucks rumbled over the rails. The noise of escaping steam filled the air. He thought: "That must be the nine o'clock just coming into the station." Why should the arrival of that particular train have any meaning for him? Suddenly a load of sadness descended upon his spirit with so crushing a weight that he leaned his head upon the table. His forehead touched the thin, blue book.

THE train drew in through the densely falling rain. The only persons on the platform were the station master with his hood pulled over his head, a porter waving a lantern, and Gradère, whose face was invisible beneath his umbrella. He walked rapidly towards a fat woman who was climbing with difficulty from a second-class compartment in which she had been the only traveler. From the third-class carriages came the clucking of a cage of chickens. This was the moment at which things were going to begin to move! To imitate Aline's voice on the telephone had been child's play. But now the difficulties were about to start. It was essential that Aline should hear his explanations. Perhaps she would refuse to listen.... If only he could have sent her a telegram saying that he would meet the train! But it would have been madness to use the Liogeats post office, and, if he had gone into Bordeaux, it would have looked strange. The telegram would have been an important piece of evidence at the inquest.... He had already risked much by telephoning that morning from Lugdunos in Aline's voice (but there had been no other way of preventing Catherine from going to the station).... No, it was better like this. The tone was what would really matter. He must be sure to get that right.

"Hullo! Yes, it's me.... Bit of a surprise, eh? Don't worry, I'll explain. Catherine's ill—running a fever...so the old man had to come clean...."

Aline, petrified with fear, listened to him in silence.

"Let's get out of the rain. I know all about everything, including that plot of theirs to get you to marry me and so leave the field clear. You needn't have gone to all that trouble, you silly old cow...I'd already made up my mind to marry you. But you were a fool, let me tell you, to mix old Desbats up in our affairs."

Aline recovered her presence of mind. She took his arm so as to get her share of the umbrella.

"They've got him to swallow that tale," she thought, "imagined it'd make things easier, I suppose. Not such a bad idea, perhaps, after all."

"I'm not sure that I'm so keen on marriage as I once was, my pet. I shall have to think it over," she said.

Gradère heaved a deep sigh. He was saved, and she was lost. He gave her ticket to the porter as he had done his own on the evening of his arrival. Then, he walked her round the back of the station.

Aline put a point-blank question:

"But why, when you knew I was coming, didn't you bring the car? There was no reason..."

"Andrès took the car and isn't back yet."

Fortunately this explanation, which had come unpremeditated to his lips, was the simplest he could have thought of, the most obvious.

Aline started to grumble: "No damn luck!" She clung to his arm, splashing her big feet in the puddles.

"A bare ten minutes' walk," he said: "I'll take you the short way."

They followed a path of trodden bark and sawdust which led between stacks of sawn planks in the direction of the town. Instead of emerging onto the road, he chose a track which skirted the outlying houses of Liogeats, and plunged into a patch of woodland. Rather imprudently he told her that this was a shortcut. There was no need for him to have said anything, for the woman had eyes only for her feet, and was concentrating her whole attention on avoiding the puddles and the ruts. It had been foolish of him to direct her attention to their surroundings. She made him raise the umbrella higher, and betrayed a certain amount of nervousness at finding that they were now among trees and at a considerable distance from any human habitation.

"This will bring us out into the avenue of the chateau," said Gabriel. "The sandy soil's a great advantage in weather like this. It positively drinks the water. I hope you see now why I avoided the road—it must be a sea of mud by this time.... Here you can keep your feet dry."

"Dry!" protested Aline breathlessly. "Why, this blasted bracken's unloading water into my shoes in spoonfuls! And it's started to rain again!"

"No, it's only the sound of the wind that makes you think that."

"God Almighty!" groaned Aline, "I'm just about fed up! My skirt's clinging to my legs. Are you sure this is the right way? Are we anywhere near the house?"

Seemingly he did not hear her, for he made no answer. They plodded on, unable to see the sandy track in the darkness, and tripping over roots which it was impossible to avoid.

"How dark it is, Gabriel. I've got a nasty feeling that we're lost.... Why don't you say something?"

She tried to free the arm which he kept tucked within his own, as he might have done had he been walking with his sweetheart. Of course they weren't lost! He was walking quickly, like a man who knows precisely where he is going, and she trotted at his side like an old and broken-winded dog. Suddenly she stopped. The twisted heels of her shoes had become fast embedded in the sand. She flung her left arm round a tree-trunk.

"Not a step further am I going!" she panted. Then, raising her hideous, husky voice, "Help!" she screamed.

But the moaning of the wind and the noise of the falling

rain drowned all other sounds. Fifty yards away not a soul could have heard her.

"You're mad!" said Gabriel in calm and level tones. "We're home. Can't you see the last of the trees, and that patch of open sky over there? That glimmer of white is the house."

She clung to her tree, getting her breath back, blinking her eyes. True enough, this *did* seem to be the end of the wood. There, where the pines stopped, must be the beginning of the garden. A white wall rose before them. Yes, it was a wall, right enough! She drank down a great gulp of air.

"What a fright you gave me, you old beast!" she said, almost affectionately. "I felt sure you hadn't forgotten the room in the Rue Lambert down in the Meriadeck quarter. Remember how I nursed you as though you'd been my own son? It cost me a pretty penny too…every penny I had…. We were in love, weren't we, Gabriel, in those days?"

She was no longer nervous, and actually led the way. She was walking as fast as she could so as to escape from her nightmare. Then, suddenly, she stopped.

"It's *not* a wall!" she moaned. "I can't see any roof or windows. Where are you taking me, darling? Where are we?"

"At the entrance to the park. We used to call this place 'The Rock' when we were children. The Du Buch girls and I used to come here often in the old days, for a tumble."

"What do you mean, tumble, Gabriel? Why tumble?"

"Come on, take a look—don't be frightened." They had reached a kind of cliff which overhung a tangled world. Because of the whiteness of the sand, Aline, in spite of the darkness, could make out a scene of miniature chaos—tiny mountains, diminutive craters.

"It's an abandoned gravel pit," Gradère explained very calmly. "We're there."

"There?" she stammered.

He had loosed his hold of her. Where could she have run to? He was perfectly easy in his mind. He could lift his paw now and let the prey scurry a stone's throw off.

"Yes, you old bitch. There was plenty of love going on in the Rue Lambert, and ever since then you've been plucking me good and proper. Oh, I'm not blaming you. Feather by feather, you did it, and now you've come to the last handful. What are you going to do with your old chicken now, my girl? After twenty-five years of it, eh?"

She swung round and started to lumber away at a jog under the trees. He made no effort to pursue her. She crashed through the dark undergrowth, and then, suddenly, fell to the earth with a sharp cry that broke off short. A long while she lay there, aping death. Not a sound could be heard but the vast rustle of the rain, the moaning of the tormented treetops and the chattering of her teeth. Perhaps he had lost track of her. Perhaps he was wandering aimlessly in the darkness. But suddenly a thin beam of light pierced the gloom, rested on her, and then went out. There was a noise of cracking branches.

His terrifying voice spoke close beside her:

"Useful things, these pocket torches, aren't they?"

Two hands seized her ankles. He harnessed himself to her body, using her legs like the shafts of a cart, and dragging her over the ground. She clung with her hands to roots and trunks and briars. A raucous sound came from her throat; she could no longer use her voice.

At last he stopped:

"Up with you, my pretty!"

She made no sign of movement, and he kicked blindly into the fleshy mass before him, on the ground. All of a sudden, it struggled to its feet. He put his arm round her waist, pressing her to him as in a dance. In the most natural way in the world, he said:

"It was just here, Aline, when we were very, very young, that I used to take the two Du Buch girls by the hand, one on each side. 'Hold tight!' I'd say, and then we'd tear down at full speed—like this."

He dragged her forward down the slope. She fell to the ground, screaming. In a wild fury, he started to roll her over and over, like a barrel, using hands and feet. By the time she reached the bottom she was suffocating and half dead. Quite calmly he dropped on her, crushing her with the full weight of his body. Then, without haste or passion, performed that act of squeezing her throat of which he had so often dreamed. A superhuman strength was in his fingers. He could have loosened them quite safely some time before he actually did so. Had it not been for the freezing rain, he would have gone on indefinitely. He would never grow weary of strangling her corpse.

He paused for breath before proceeding to the last stage of his task. He had not a dry spot on him. He was a sodden mass of rain and sweat. He made sure that no one had moved the planks which, the evening before, he had laid across the entrance to a cave which workmen, in the old days, had used as a shelter. He scrambled into the hole, and switched on his pocket-torch. The damned rain had seeped through somehow, and collected in the excavation he had made here in readiness. "This'll be the last bath she'll ever take," he thought. How tired he felt all of a sudden. He clambered once more between the shafts, harnessing himself to her not yet rigid legs. The load he dragged behind him now no longer struggled. She had lost one of her shoes, and he had to go back to look for it with his torch. He mustn't go further until he had found it.... Ah, there it was, with its twisted heel....

The effort demanded of him now was nothing compared with his labors of the previous night. Digging a hole is what takes it out of a man, not filling it in. All the same, the work left him breathless. His arms felt as heavy as lead, his legs ached. There had been some rotting straw and dead bracken across the hole, and this covering he now replaced.... No one ever came to this hide-out.... What about the spade? He took the handle out and buried it. He would throw the head into a deep pool that he had marked down in the Balion. No one would think of looking for it there.... What agony it was climbing the slope again! The rain was still falling. Gradère used the last ounce of his strength in an effort to reach the top. It was as though someone were leading him.

Everything was over and done with now...never again would he need anyone. He walked through the drenched darkness, pressing the head of the spade to his side till it cut his fingers. He turned into the road along which he had walked in the moonlight on the evening of his arrival. All that remained of that world of appearances now was the clinging mud and the endless, enveloping rain. He reached the bridge over the Balion. Once more he had to scramble down, sinking up to his ankles in the sodden grass, pulling his feet free of the mud with a sucking sound. He flung the spade into the stream, and regained the road. Already the physical marks of crime were upon him. He was emptied of his hatred. For a quarter of a century it had accumulated within him, drop by drop, and now, in a second, it was gone.

How well he used to sleep when he was twenty, in that room in the Rue Lambert! Still, in imagination, he could see the torn wallpaper with the patches of dried blood where mosquitoes and bugs had been crushed. It had been his custom to wait until Aline's "clients" had left before going to warm himself at her fire.... So what? He had killed her in order to avoid being killed himself. What point was there in trying to find excuses? But the violence of crime no longer buoyed him. Little by little a hideous fear began to dominate the confusion of his thoughts. A sense of solitude, such as he had never known before, weighed him down. He was alone now. What had become of the hot fire within him? Where, now, was the unseen guide, the insidious voice, the ever-present counsel? Up to now he had acted like a blind man, had merely had to hold fast to the lead and let the dog pull him. But now the dog had broken the lead: the eyes of the blind had been opened. He could see even in the dark. Nothing now but to wait until the alarm was raised. The hunt would soon be on. The hounds, with their noses to the ground, would be baying, and coming nearer and nearer. The first sign would be a few lines in the paper, references to a "wanted" witness. There would be talk of a police inquiry. He would be questioned—for an hour, for two hours, for a whole night. Relay after relay of torturers. They would get him at last by a process of sheer exhaustion. In a flash all his life would be revealed, all his hideous life. Andrès would know! But if Aline's little plan had come off, he would have been found out in any case.

But for the unceasing rain he would have turned in by the roadside. The Presbytery! If only he could pluck up courage to knock at that door! Soaked to the skin, he crouched in the porch, his hands timidly stroking the doorstep. He touched it as he might have done a face, feeling its wrinkles beneath his fingers.

1.

⬦

The house was fast asleep: He held his shoes in his hand—two solid lumps of mud. A streak of light was showing under his door. Had he left a light burning? He went in. Somebody was kneeling in front of Adila's little collection of sacred objects.

Mathilde got up and looked at him without saying a word. It was enough for him that she was there. He was shivering.

"I'm cold. Let me get into bed."

He spoke as one asking a favor. He might have been taken for a beggar. He pulled off his drenched clothes. She turned away her head. She could smell the mingled stench of damp wool and sweat. He had pulled the eiderdown up to his chin, and she could see nothing but a head with chattering teeth and a frizz of white hair.

"You must take my shoes, get the mud off them, and hide my clothes."

She found her tongue at last: What had he done? Where had he been?

"Over at the Rock," he answered. "Do you remember? I used to take Adila and you by the hand." Then, suddenly lowering his voice, "It was in self-defense. A man's got a right to save his own skin, hasn't he?"

His tone was that of a suppliant. The face that emerged from the sheets was the face of an old man.

"So, I'm your accomplice?" Mathilde voiced her feeling as a question; then, in sudden bewilderment, "Am I really your accomplice? Of course I am, since I knew…"

"Nobody saw us. She's been living in furnished rooms. She had had a quarrel with her landlady and never told her where she was going. The woman will find Symphorien's letters, but there's nothing to tell where they came from, and, anyhow, she's the last person in the world likely to stick her nose into any business that looks like turning into a scandal. You could persuade her to keep her mouth shut. Aline was on her own…utterly alone. They'll look for her, I expect they'll ask me questions…but that won't get them far. I've been here the whole time.…"

"What about the Marquis de Dorth?" Mathilde inquired sharply. "It was he who staged the whole thing, and he must have known about her projected trip. He'll talk to the police, and you know how he hates you.…"

Gabriel choked back a cry and sat up in bed. How *could* he have forgotten the Marquis!

"He's got no proof.… I'll deny everything."

Mathilde shrugged her shoulders.

"Do you really think they won't pick up the scent? She was probably seen taking her ticket. One always is—someone always sees one."

"I'm not going to budge," he stammered, "I shall go to ground here and wait...."

Mathilde sat down on the bed. Without looking at him, she asked:

"What have you done with her?"

"We had a quarrel. She came here with the object of putting me down, didn't she? I never meant...but when I heard her talking so cynically, well, I just saw red."

He was lying, even at this stage, defending himself, trying to find extenuating circumstances.

"I was unarmed. Isn't that proof enough?"

"But why did you take a spade with you when you went out last night?"

He looked at her with terror and hatred in his eyes.

"So you were spying on me too, like the rest of them! Going to give me away, are you? Better look out, my girl!"

She raised a finger to her lips. The sound of a smothered sneeze had come from the corridor. She half opened the door.

"Is that you, Catherine? Gabriel came along to look for me—he's got a violent fever. I'm going to cup him. The things are in your father's room, I think. Could you get them without waking him?"

Gradère heard Catherine's voice:

"He seemed perfectly all right today."

"He went to bed immediately after dinner. He's running a temperature."

Catherine said that she would go and look for the cupping glasses. The door remained ajar. Gradère heaved a sigh of relief.... Mathilde was playing up, was beginning to lie. She put his wet clothes on the radiator in the dressing room.

Catherine came back with the glasses. Mathilde thanked her through the slit of the half-opened door, waited until she had gone off down the corridor, and then, spreading a newspaper on the floor, began to scrape the mud from his shoes with an old metal paper knife.

When Gabriel stammered out a few words of thanks, she said harshly:

"It's for Andrès' sake."

Whether it was or wasn't, what did it matter? He was no longer alone. For the moment he was nothing at all, a mere discarded rag.

"What are you going to do? I suppose you had some sort of a plan?" She fired the question at him point blank.

Of course he had a plan—to frighten the old man, frighten him to death—and he wasn't joking!

"Aline just wouldn't have turned up, and, as she never answered his letters, he wouldn't have had a scrap of evidence against me. But he'd have felt that I was top dog, that it was I who was calling the tune, and he wouldn't have been able to stick it."

Mathilde shrugged: what a childish scheme! Anyhow, the situation was just as he'd planned, wasn't it? In what way was it different?

"It's I who am different, Mathilde.... This business has shaken me up.... It wasn't childish at all. I'd have had him where I wanted him in next to no time, and without having to lay a finger on him."

"And do you really think I'd have stood by and done nothing?"

She realized that this protest had come rather too late in the day. Not that it mattered now. Symphorien was safe. The man with the chattering teeth couldn't harm a fly.

He was regaining his self-confidence, and began to rehearse their next moves.

"You made me go to bed immediately after dinner. You've been here looking after me, haven't, so to speak, left me for a moment. There's a pretty good chance that Catherine never heard me go out. Gercinthe's as deaf as a post, and the maids sleep down at the farm. I was careful not to use the main entrance of the station, and I'm pretty sure that no one recognized me with my umbrella open. The station master and the porter both had their hoods up, and weren't bothering about anything except getting in out of the rain...."

As she listened to him she was conscious of a vague feeling of disappointment. What had she expected of this coward? Faced by this simulacrum of a man, what was it she missed? She had depended on him. He had always seemed so strong, had held the promise of such happiness. He had led her through pleasant ways; not that she had been guilty of any serious misdemeanour, anything she need mention in confession. Still, the goal to which he had pointed had appeared to her as lovely beyond imagining. Was it really the fact of his crime that she held against him now?

Would she have despised him quite so much as she did if he had returned as a conqueror glorying in what he had done? Wasn't it the beaten creature rather than the criminal whom she held in horror?

"Something has just occurred to me, Mathilde. I remember, now. She never had any personal contact with the

Marquis de Dorth. She told me herself that their relations were very complicated because of his dread of scandal. They always communicated through a third party. We can be easy in our minds where he's concerned. *He* won't give anything away...."

"What's the good of worrying our heads about it?" she interrupted in a hard voice: "The only thing we can do is wait and see. If nothing happens, life will go on just as though you had never come back to Liogeats.... It's odd the picture I had of you. Of course, I always knew the kind of man you were, but I see now that I thought you strong and resourceful; I was a fool! Whatever it is that you have done tonight (I don't want to know: I don't believe a single word you have told me, and I forbid you to mention the subject in my hearing)...whatever it is, the fact remains that you're the kind of man who thinks only of his own skin, who can't stand up to danger, who loses his head as soon as things get difficult...a poor skunk, when all's said!"

Gradère was sitting on the bed. He looked at her in silence. Let her abuse him as much as she liked. He was no longer cold, and was beginning to feel reassured. If the worst came to the worst, Mathilde's evidence would save him. The color crept back into his cheeks: his sense of numbness was slowly wearing off. The reptile, safe once more in its hole, safe and warm, darted its tiny, silver-crested head above the blankets.

He had reacted violently to Mathilde's contempt. His understanding of the situation had been correct. She had snapped at the hook with a greediness that surprised even him. Well, she shouldn't, she mustn't, be disappointed. He would tread his chosen road. Everything that this woman expected of him he would accomplish. Fortunately, she had shown no sign of tenderness. Had she done so it would merely have added to his terror and intensified his weakness. Her contemptuous pity, on the other hand, had the effect of driving him forward, made it possible for him to overcome the almost sexual exhaustion which had followed his performance of the act. Aline's death was of no importance whatever. Of that he was sure. A filthy, drunken old hag had been swept into nothingness, that was all. The snake had swallowed the toad. What larger place in the order of the universe did the night's execution occupy than that? He had, no doubt, brought to it rather more passion than he should have done; still, after all, one can hardly be expected to do away with a woman in cold blood.

"My dear Mathilde," he said, after a prolonged silence, "you are condemning me for a weakness that is purely physical. Rest assured: we shall go on now to the very end."

She protested with violence: Why did he say "we"? What had she got to do with all this?

"Like all women, my pet, you are a hypocrite. But I don't care. Hypocrite or not, you have revived my sense of responsibility…that's the honest truth—responsibility to you and to Andrès."

He pretended not to hear her protests, but went on:

"For the moment we must wait. How we act must be dictated by circumstances. If nothing floats to the surface, we shall have them where we want them, and soon, too. If I am questioned, I shall wriggle out, thanks to you. Forewarned is forearmed."

Mathilde put a question in a low voice:

"Isn't there a danger that they may find...that they may find the spot where she is? No, don't tell me! All I mean is, are you easy on that point?"

A ghost of a smile showed on his lips.

"'No places,' he said, "seem so mysterious, so hidden, as those in which we played as children. Don't you remember how appalled we were when we discovered a bird snare on that 'desert island' in the middle of the Balion which we used to call the Beauty Spot? Well, the reason that the place where she is seems to me to be so inaccessible is precisely because nothing, so far as I know, has ever happened there since the days when I used to take you and Adila by the hand, and pull you down the slope...."

"The Rock," said Mathilde very quietly.

"Yes, the Rock: a place of burial of which she was unworthy. It is we, the three of us, who ought to be lying there in the sand that once felt so soft and warm to our bare feet. We must just wait. But I can't be everywhere. You must keep an eye on Andrès for me...he makes me uneasy."

"He's the same as he always is."

"His is a very simple, an animal, nature (I use the word in no derogatory sense). He is one of those who, when they are in love, are least able to stand up to the idea of separation, to the idea of *suppression*, one of those, more especially, who have no fear of death, because death has no meaning for them except the meaning that they happen to want at the moment—that of a condition in which they will no longer be conscious of the irreparable absence of the loved one. That is why you have got to keep an eye on him."

Mathilde, her hand on the latch, turned round to say:

"I probably know him better than you do. He may, I don't deny it, have had a disappointment that strikes at him through the senses. But I confess that the idea of him as a passionate man makes me smile! That's the point. How dare you, tonight of all nights..."

Only when she had gone did Gradère realize that he had, in fact, been speaking of Andrès as though nothing had happened. Things are rarely important in themselves. The essential thing, if ever he should find the hounds of justice at his heels, was to maintain an attitude of easy detachment...

The deep sleep into which he fell almost at once was the measure of his weariness. At that moment, not Aline's body could have been so blind, so deaf, as this exhausted man, lying with his head thrown back and his mouth open. His hands, which he had not even bothered to wash, were crossed upon his breast.

16.

IT was young Lassus who brought the note from the curé.

Gradère carefully scrutinized the maid's face—the first
he had seen that day. There was nothing unusual about it. He
felt reassured, but the letter made him uneasy. What a fool he
had been, in the present circumstances, to put himself at the
mercy of this priest, and, especially, to do so out of the confessional. Still, the secrecy of confession covers any confidence
that a priest may receive *qua* priest. He was not really afraid
that the man might turn evidence against him. Nevertheless,
the thought of opening the envelope filled him with a sense
of repugnance. Had he not, perhaps, better just send a word
to the writer that he had received his communication, and
leave it at that? All the same, he decided to read the contents.
It would be nothing but a lot of honeyed phrases—the kind
of thing that priests always write.

"No matter how guilty a life may be, it can never surprise
a man who knows men! We should feel astonished at nothing, my dear sir, save at that mystery by virtue of which you
have only to tell over again, on your knees, all that your little

exercise book contains, for the last grain of the huge block that weighs you down to vanish, for there to be no difference between your soul and that of a little child, except for the presence of a few scars. You are *not* damned. No human being is damned. You must realize the astonishing nature of that grace whose beneficiary you are. Just think for a moment. The pious for the most part live and die in the odor of sanctity without ever knowing more of the supernatural than is revealed to them by Faith. How different is your case! If it be true that the Enemy of God and man really exists, then it is true that everything else exists too. How can you not kneel in thankfulness? The story of your wife, Adila, through whom salvation may come to you, has opened my eyes, the eyes of an unworthy priest whom the reading of your exercise book (I confess it with shame) at first so sorely troubled. We must look to our end, for only our death can shed light upon our life. That poor woman attained to the heights because you had dragged her into the depths. But for her sin, would she ever have shown the measure of her virtue? Do you realize (but of course you do, for you have made it abundantly plain) that you have been, that you are, to all eternity, the husband of a martyr and a saint?"

The further he read the more did Gradère feel rising within him that rage which he could never for long suppress. At the words *saint* and *martyr* he could read no further, but tore the letter into fragments and threw them into the grate. Standing in front of the mirror, he studied his reflection, the reflection of a sickly-looking man in pajamas with tousled hair. He was breathing hard. There was a bronchial roughness in the sound. Still, there was nothing seriously wrong with the old carcass. Life was once more flowing in his veins—and more than life, a mysterious renewal of youth. He felt himself to be capable of anything. He could carry through any enterprise to success. When Mathilde entered the room she was surprised to find him up and dressed and ready for battle. He thumped his chest with his fists. His voice, when he spoke, was bouyant:

"A man risen from the dead, eh, old girl?"

She did not answer him but turned away. There was a look upon her face of bitterness and despair. She had not slept. Her cheeks were mottled with yellow patches.

"If you had been ill, I would have looked after you," she said at length. "But since you are perfectly hale and hearty it is as well I should tell you that I shall never again set foot in this room, and want no more confidences from you. All I can do is to ignore, is to forget, everything I know. May God have mercy on me! From now on, don't expect me to stir a finger...."

"So now, just when the goal's in sight, you've gone soft?"

"What can I possibly have in common with you? There is no 'goal' for me."

Just as she reached the door he said in a low voice:

"Andrès."

She turned on him in a fury:

"You have stolen him from me! I have lost him, yes, lost him! He was my son, my much loved child. Then you came, and troubled what hitherto had been pure. You have poisoned all of us. Now he flees from me. There can no longer be any doubt of that. This very morning I tried to go into his room, but he turned me out. The sight of me is horrible to him. I can guess what you have been saying about me—the things at which you hinted one evening in my hearing, the things that lurk beneath your every lying word.... We daren't any longer look at one another...and now, of all times, when he feels threatened by what, at any moment, may emerge into the light of day—because, have no doubt of it, your crime *will* be discovered. Murderers always are discovered!"

Gradère took her by the arm and shook her:

"Shut up! Someone will hear. Anyhow, what of it? Didn't I act perfectly legitimately in self-defense? You fool! Do you really think that the only crimes are the ones you read of in the newspapers? Have you any idea of the number of murderers that go unpunished? I have. There are many more fish in the sea than ever get into the snares and the nets set by the police. You've no idea how many there are (myriads!) darting about in the depths, out of all danger of being caught."

She was not listening to him, though she still stood by the door, clutching her old purple dressing gown about her heavy, handsome body. There was a fixed stare in her eyes. She shook her head and stammered:

"I didn't want...I didn't want...I can't understand how... and with no one to help me...no one...."

"No one to help you?"

In gentler mood he looked at her now with an expression of mournful irony.

"No one to help you?" he said again. "How blind you are!"

She thought that he was speaking of himself, and protested that she wanted no more connivance between them, that she repulsed with loathing everything he was suggesting, that her only feeling for him was one of horror. Perhaps she hoped that he would strike her. But he said, in the same calm tone, that it was of somebody else he was thinking:

"You would do well to remember the text which says, 'In your midst is someone whom you know not.' You seem to forget that I was brought up in a seminary. Here, in Liogeats, is someone whom you know not of. Go and look for him. You have my full permission to tell him everything, see? Even what happened last night."

She felt sure that his mind must be wandering. But when, in a colorless voice, he mentioned the name of the Abbé Forcas, she looked uneasy.

"It's a very bad sign," she said, "if *you've* begun to like *him*."

"Fool!" he muttered between his teeth, then, on a sudden, burst out furiously:

"You're right, *don't* go! I don't know what I can have been thinking of! He's the laughing-stock of the place, bent double under a load of ridicule and shame. He's a coward: They spit at him and he says nothing. They could lead him to the slaughter-house and not a bleat would he utter! They lay upon him all the filthy acts of their own secret lives, and he consents to carry the load. Even if he *is* tempted to answer back that *he's* not the one who is guilty, he, a mere rag of a man, a poor butt at whom every one laughs, he doesn't yield, but prefers to say nothing. Alone in his church he mutters his prayers—and his good parishioners, you among them, flee from him, and despise him. His very superiors are filled with suspicion because he is an object of scandal.... What's that?" he passed his hand over his eyes in a bewildered fashion. "What's that you said?"

But he saw that Mathilde had left the room.

17.

ON Thursday evening the train was very late. It was almost
ten o'clock when, at last, Desbats heard the long expected
puffing, the sharp hiss of escaping steam. There was a scream
of wheels coming to a stop on the rails. In twenty minutes'
time Aline would mount the steps. In an hour all would be
over. Did Gradère suspect anything? According to Catherine,
no one ever saw him now, except at meals. But he was not
the man to let the noose be drawn round his neck without
putting up a fight. Once he realized that he had lost, there
was no knowing what he might not do.

The old man was trembling with fear. We believe that
when we have planned something carefully enough it will
turn out exactly as we intended: but only too often it shows
a strange and hostile face, so that we do not recognize it....
Gradère would be caught in his sleep. All that instinct of
divination which is bred in such men by necessity would go
for nothing.

Desbats went to the window and drew the curtain aside.
But the outside shutters were closed, and the effort to shift

them was too much for him. He opened the door and went on to the landing, which was dimly lit by the hanging lamp in the hall, descended the stairs a little way, and leaned over the banisters. He saw Andrès sitting by the table on which some magazines lay in a pile, his arms crossed on the open page of one of them, his face hidden in his hands. He went back to his armchair. His breath came gaspingly, not because of the movement he had just made, but because of his terror of what was yet to come. Steps sounded outside the front door, and he thought he should die of fright. He scrambled to his feet once again and stood leaning against the back of the chair. Catherine came in. She was alone.

"There was no one at the station," she said, taking off her coat.

"Are you sure you looked everywhere? The old drunkard may have been at the bottle. She may have fallen asleep...."

Catherine assured him that she had looked into every carriage. The Firsts and Seconds had been completely empty.

Desbats breathed again. The fateful moment had receded: nothing would happen tonight. His courage returned.

"She must be ill—that's the obvious explanation. But I'm surprised she didn't send a wire. She may have thought it would be unwise. With a woman like that one can never be sure. Don't you agree, my dear?"

He noticed that Catherine was looking sullen and thoughtful. Suddenly he burst out with:

"You know something!"

She made a gesture of denial, but without much conviction. He pressed her to speak.

"Don't fuss, don't get into a state," she muttered. "Promise me you'll be sensible and not excite yourself."

She could no longer conceal her anxiety.

"All right, then, I'll tell you…. The train was very late and I got talking with several people who had come down for papers…in particular, with Mademoiselle Pibeste from the post office."

She paused. She could hear her father's wheezing breath. She ought to have screwed herself up to say nothing…but now she had started, the sooner she got it over and done with the better.

"I happened to say something about telephone calls from Paris, and she remarked that she didn't often have occasion…"

Symphorien had guessed. By the time she went on he had taken the full force of the blow.

"Nobody rang me up from Paris last Monday. I was speaking to the Lugdunos exchange."

For some moments the old man could say nothing. He murmured, "But the voice…the hoarse voice…." Catherine shrugged her shoulders. Had he forgotten that Andrès had once told them, speaking of his father, that he could mimic all of them to perfection—that it was really "killing"?

"But…but…you mean she may have arrived on Monday night? That's nonsense. He probably sent her a wire from Lugdunos telling her not to come, signed with my name…."

"That's certainly a possibility," Catherine replied. But he saw that she did not believe what she was saying. She half opened the door. A faint sound was coming from the ground floor.

"It's Andrès: he's filling cartridges," she muttered. "We'd better keep a careful watch on him, too. I said as much to

Mamma this evening, and do you know what her answer was? That he was avoiding her, that she had only to go into a room where he was for him to leave it...."

"Your mother..." Desbats broke in.

"I know all about my mother! She's the one who gave the show away. That'll teach you," said Catherine in a furious voice.

There was a long silence, at the end of which she added, more quietly:

"On Monday night and in the early hours of Tuesday morning she was in Gradère's room. Her excuse was that she was nursing him. He was ill—or so she told me, and I must admit that, so far as I could see from the landing, he did look very flushed and feverish. I had to go and fetch the cupping glasses."

"If he had gone out after dinner, would you have heard him?"

"Not necessarily.... Remember, we had let ourselves get rather slack that evening. I was so glad not to have to go to the station through that awful downpour."

The old man put a question: "What's your own private opinion?"

She made a vague, outward gesture with her hands, but said nothing.

"If that woman really did get here on Monday evening, according to plan..."

Symphorien Desbats broke off, trying to read the expression on his daughter's face. The silence of the winter's night wrapped them round. Catherine wanted to help her father into bed as she always did, but he would not let her. He refused to lie down, and seemed as panicky as a child. Indeed, when next he spoke it was in an almost childish whimper:

"Someone's coming upstairs."

Catherine was in a mood to grumble:

"How nervy you are!"

She set the door ajar.

"It's Mamma going to bed. No, I was wrong, she's coming in here."

"I must be ready for her," muttered Symphorien.

As she came into the room, they both remained silent, astonished by what they saw. The familiar face was like a stranger's. The eyes were those of a sleep-walker and there were patches of bilious pallor on the cheeks. Her hair was half down, and a pin slipped from it on to the floor.

"Catherine dear, you *must* find some excuse to sit with Andrès for a bit. Try to make him talk—if necessary, say something that will annoy him and put him in a temper. This mulish silence of his is getting on my nerves."

"Stay with him yourself, and leave Catherine be!" Desbats broke out. "I suppose there's no need for anyone to stay with *me*! I'm threatened as much as anybody else—as you ought to know, none better—you…you…fraud!"

He had half risen from his chair, his hands gripping the arms. Then he let himself fall back.

Mathilde seemed not to have heard him. She was still pleading with her daughter:

"Do please go, dear, and look after Andrès. I'll take your place with your father."

"No! No!" screamed the old man. "I know how it is: you want to hand me over to…"

The words poured from his lips in a confusion of rage and terror. Catherine hesitated, then moved towards the door.

"I shall never again know any peace of mind," she said at length, to her mother, "after what you've done. Who'd ever have thought that you would side with *that* man!"

"But, Catherine, he's Andrès' father...."

"What of it? We only meant to get him out of the house, didn't we? That would have put an end to the whole business, I and Andrès would have been the gainer."

"There's a great deal you don't know, my dear," said Mathilde in a determined voice. "It wasn't *only* that. They wanted to do for him...that creature would have handed him over....I dreaded the scandal for Andrès' sake. I thought I was doing only my duty. I didn't know that, by acting as I did, I was exposing him to a still worse danger. I thought that if I warned him he would clear out, that we should be quit of him, that he would manage to hide somewhere. I couldn't foresee..."

She was suddenly aware of two faces turned towards her, of two pairs of eyes fastened on her lips, of two people waiting on tenterhooks for what she was about to reveal. She passed a hand over her forehead:

"No, really, I don't know a thing—no more than you do. That's the truth, I swear it. I'm just frightened. I've got an idea...."

She dropped into a chair. The others waited for her to continue, but she sat on in a stupor, barely noticing that Catherine was deep in a whispered argument with her father.

"You gave me your word that all you cared about was getting him out of the house."

"How was I to know what that woman planned to do with him? It was no concern of mine: it didn't interest me."

"Anything that has to do with Andrès is a matter of concern."

"Speak for yourself, you little fool!"

Catherine turned to her mother and, raising her voice, said:

"All right, Mamma: you stay here while I go and see what's happening downstairs."

"I forbid you to leave me alone," shouted her father, but she pretended not to hear. She hurried down, lit the hanging lamp in the hall, crossed the dining room, the door of which had remained open, and went into the small room which was always jokingly referred to in the Du Buch family as "the Arsenal," because the sporting guns and ammunition were kept there.

Hanging on racks against the wall were guns of every kind, ranging from the old "muzzle-loader" with which the elder Gradère had never missed a woodcock, to Grandpapa Du Buch's Lefaucheux, and the latest pattern of "hammerless."

Seated at the deal table, Andrès was busy filling cartridge cases with powder and shot. He glanced up at the sound of somebody entering the room, but made no further sign of interest. His face looked drawn: his mouth was tight shut, and his eyes had a withdrawn expression—the kind of expression that one sees in animals when they are off their feed.

"The wind's gone round since this morning," said Catherine. "We can go out after woodcock tomorrow.... Make me up some cartridges, will you?"

He glanced at the great standing press, the doors of which were open.

"There's more than enough here," he said, in apathetic tones.

"Of course, if it'll be a bore for you having me come along..."

He shrugged his shoulders:

"I don't give a damn whether you come or don't," he growled.

Not a muscle of her face moved. He had interrupted what he was doing, and sat there playing with an empty cartridge case. In a sudden burst of ill-temper he said:

"Why are you looking at me like that?"

"I put up with a lot of things, Andrès, and I don't suppose I've always been a very pleasant sort of person.... It's my duty to put up with a lot of things..."

"All of us..."

"But what I can't put up with is seeing you suffer...."

She began to cry. She looked, suddenly, like the skinny little girl he had been so fond of teasing in the old days. He had forgotten she could look like that, so accustomed had he grown to her sullen or her mocking moods. He tried to find something to say, and she realized with amazement that he was not going to snub her.

"Don't make yourself miserable on my account," he brought out at last. "Nothing matters to me any more."

Then, probably for the first time in all the years they had lived together in the same house, she heard him enunciate a criticism of life.

"Everything's foul—don't you agree?"

Was it only the woman he loved of whom he was thinking? He should feel some concern, too, for his wretched father. He must have had a terrible shock, thought Catherine, but what had happened to make him avoid Tamati as he was doing?

He broke his silence to say: "But when there's nothing left—are you afraid of death, Catherine?"

"For myself—no. For others—yes."

Suddenly she sat down by him and put her arm in his.

"No! Andrès, no! Promise me. Swear to me!" Her voice was urgent.

He was surprised by her eagerness, surprised and somewhat upset. He did not repel her. It came over him that, when all was said and done, she was a woman. Some instinct made her remove her arm. She went across and leaned against the wall at the other side of the table on which Andrès had now put his elbows, and was sitting with his head in his hands. Behind him the barrels of the shotguns gave off a faint gleam. There was a pervading smell of grease.

"I want to ask you to forgive me," said the girl at last. "I've been wicked and odious…yes, I have…but you must make an effort to understand my feelings. You see, the way you and my mother have always treated me as though I really didn't exist at all, was more than I could bear. You'll never know.… But that's all over now, as you'll see. Everything I have, everything I ever shall have, is for you only.…"

The face he raised to hers showed complete bewilderment. He protested that he didn't care two hoots about what she had or what she would have.… Everyone believed that was all he ever thought about, that he was like the rest of them and cared for nothing but the land. His father knew to his cost how little he really bothered about it.

"It's only natural that I should feel attached to the place. No one else knows every inch of it as I do. I've surveyed all the boundaries, and none of the neighbors dare alter them so long as I'm around. I know the farmers too and they know me. I'm far from being their enemy. Like them I know what it is to work for others. Fundamentally there is no difference between them and me. But as for the pleasure of saying to myself, 'That's *mine*,' you'd be surprised, my poor child, if you really knew how little I care. I've got other things to bother about."

"Other things?" said Catherine, and the old, ill-natured note had come back into her voice. "What you mean is another person. But I'm not blaming you," she hurriedly added. "You see, I understand that, too."

He shrugged, and the gesture expressed weariness.

"You're on quite the wrong tack. If I were carefree enough to think about that person, I shouldn't be complaining like this, because in that case I shouldn't feel that I'd lost anything…" (he hesitated, seeming to fumble for his words). "How can I explain what I mean? There have been times when unhappiness of quite a different kind has floored me… there have been times when a certain kind of pain can actually seem like pleasure. I won't pretend that I haven't suffered abominably because of her…forgive me for being so frank.…"

"There's nothing to forgive," she said quietly. "It's all perfectly simple. You're not telling me anything I didn't know already."

He went on:

"But something else has come between me and my suffering—that particular suffering…"

On a sudden impulse he got up and took her arm: "You're mixed up in all this business, Catherine. Tell me, what's going on in this house?"

The question threw her into confusion, and she made no answer.

"You see, you can't deny it."

Then, in almost the identical terms that old Desbats had used a while back, "You know something," he said. "Tell me what you know."

Little used though he was to reading facial expression, he saw in the eyes before him, for all her effort to conceal it, a look of compassion that brought him up short.

"You won't tell me?"

But he did not press his question, perhaps he was terrified of what her answer might be. He sat down again at the table and began to play with the empty cartridge cases. Standing at a little distance, Catherine followed with her eyes the movements of his powerful hands.

Suddenly, he started to speak again:

"You've realized what he means to me—haven't you? You hate and despise him, but I loved him, in spite of all of you. I used to think of his life of love and happiness, which is so different from our lives. Everything that *your* father hoards, he has squandered on pleasure. You'll probably think me mad when I tell you that I looked on my father as a younger brother. He has stripped me of everything, but if I had more I would willingly give it to him. It's not that I'm good, but simply that I believed him when he said that he would repay me a hundredfold. I had come to rely on him. I knew that only by learning the lessons he has taught me could I ever hope to be loved, could I ever hope to be more than a miserable worm. I believed that he was fond of me...and not selfishly, like Tamati...that he wanted my happiness. I tell you all this, and probably I don't make myself at all plain.... I always knew he had been a bad lot...and I admired him for it. A bad lot? Yes, a man who had spent his whole life in love affairs...in unimaginable orgies...well, for an unlinked cub like me, that at least..."

Catherine was holding her breath, fearing to interrupt him. She kept her eyes averted.

"But there were certain words that I understood only too well, insults muttered by Uncle Symphorien...certain allusions. I buried them deep inside me, I wouldn't let myself think of them. All the same, I realized clearly enough what people in Liogeats were saying about him.... And then, quite suddenly the other evening, when he said something to me so extraordinary that you couldn't even imagine what it was, so extraordinary that I didn't really understand what he meant...quite suddenly I found myself seeing and hearing a man whom I didn't know, a man in whose existence I didn't believe. In a flash, I saw him with your eyes, with the eyes of everyone in this house. What a revelation! From that moment, everything that I had so wilfully ignored, deliberately refused to see, became crystal clear and full of meaning. I've become like a dog who snuffs the ground and is terrified of the scent he picks up. We're all in this thing together—only I'm the one person who is playing his part in the dark."

She came close and, with her arms round his neck, gently stroked his hair, as she might have done to calm a frightened animal. So little did he attempt to resist her, that now, when he was at the very peak of suffering, she felt for the first time a woman's joy, a mysterious feeling of uneasy peace. She grew more daring, and pressed the great curly head against her shoulder.

"Much sadness may come because of him," she said in a low voice. "It will come, but it will pass." There was an ardent, odd, eagerness in her tone: "Because you will lay your head on my breast and find a hiding place within my arms."

He freed himself, but quite gently.

"I don't love you, Catherine," he said. "I never could love you as you want to be loved."

She did not move, but stood there with her eyes closed and her arm bent as though it were still about his neck. She was waiting until she should feel strong enough to answer him calmly:

"I know that, but it doesn't matter so long as I am here to watch over you."

He was not listening to her now, but gazing into the distance. Suddenly, he asked her a question:

"Have you ever thought that he might be mad? My father, I mean. He behaves so extravagantly at times."

Catherine dared not ask, "How do you mean? What does he do?" She would have liked to change the subject, but Andrés had become unusually talkative:

"I can only make you understand if I first confess something. I realize now how idiotic it was, but I *did* mean to disappear. No, let me go on…it'll probably give you a good laugh! To cut a long story short, I planned to make myself ill…you know how easily I do get ill. I had pleurisy once, like my father, and at the same age. Don't you remember that Clairac wanted to send me to hospital? Well, the other night, when it was raining cats and dogs—please don't laugh—the idea came to me that I would stay out in the downpour as long as possible with nothing on but a shirt. I did it two nights running. It was horrible. Then I came in, and went out on the balcony. The only result was a cold in the head, so I gave up the whole silly scheme. Next time I want…"

"You won't want anything of the sort ever again, promise me you won't, Andrès?"

He ignored this appeal, and went on playing with the cartridges scattered over the table.

"Well, you won't believe it, but I saw my father go out each of those nights—or at least the ones I spent on the balcony. The rain was terrific—you remember how awful the weather was? It was Saturday—no, Sunday and Monday. I heard him go out by the back door into the yard."

"But you didn't see him? You couldn't have seen him. You couldn't have known it actually *was* he."

She spoke without emphasis. He did not notice that the color had drained from her cheeks, or the odd way in which she was leaning against the wall.

"I know that, but I recognized his step. Besides, who else would have been likely to leave the house at that time of night? I went along and knocked at his door, but there was no answer. And I heard him come back through all that rain. Next morning he must have gone out again and stayed away all day—because he got home about midnight. What a running to and fro there was. You went past my door twice...."

"Yes, he was ill, and in no state to put his nose out of doors. I swear that's true."

"He had better luck than I had, and didn't get drenched for nothing. Don't you think he *must* be mad to go running about the countryside in weather like that? It's easy to guess there was a woman in the case. But if he had wanted to meet her, he surely could have chosen some more convenient moment. I suppose the truth is that he goes dashing about all night in Paris, and sleeps during the day, and couldn't resist the temptation to do the same sort of thing in Liogeats. What's wrong, Catherine?"

She had fallen into a chair and sat there rigid.

"It wasn't him, Andrès," she stammered: "you *mustn't* have seen him, you *didn't* see him. You heard no one leave the house on those two nights. Promise me you didn't...."

All of a sudden her white little face fell sideways on to her right shoulder.

"Catherine! What's the matter?"

He took her in his arms, and laid her on an old broken-down divan on which they had been accustomed to have wrestling matches when they were children. Almost at once she opened her eyes, and fixed them on Andrès who was kneeling beside her, holding her hand.

"Swear to me that what you heard, and what you saw shall remain a secret between us!"

She sat up, listening intently. A clamor of angry voices had broken out on the bedroom floor.

"Don't go," she begged. "Don't, Andrès!"

But he pushed her aside, and took the stairs two at a time. Old Desbats, in a dressing gown, was leaning against the landing wall, fighting for breath. Gradère, his hands in his pockets, was chuckling and shrugging his shoulders, while Mathilde, in a white heat of fury, was saying:

"You slipped into my husband's room with the object of frightening him, of making him ill with fright…and when I say, make ill…what a vile creature you are!"

He tried to drown her voice:

"Why so indignant, my dear? Why all this play-acting?"

"Look out!" cried Catherine. "Andrès is there!"

Mathilde, clutching her old purple wrap about her, turned towards the young man, her face puffy with crying. He hung back slightly, standing on one of the treads of the staircase, leaning on the banisters.

"I can't help that," she moaned. "He's got to know sooner or later, he's got to understand…"

Catherine cut her short:

"Why did you leave Papa? I begged you not to leave him alone."

"He sent me out of the room, Catherine; he wouldn't have me there. Fortunately, I didn't go back to bed."

At last old Desbats managed to find his voice:

"How do I know you didn't let him in? Haven't you played traitor once already? You're accessory to whatever it was that happened the other night…you're on his side…on the murderer's side!"

Catherine's strident tones rang out again:

"Can't you see that Andrès is there?"

The altercation stopped suddenly. Every eye was fixed on

Andrès, who was still clinging motionless to the banisters, and breathing hard, like a bull when, with the sword in his flank, he trembles on his legs but does not fall. Only Gradère kept his back to him.

The boy went up to his father and touched him on the shoulder: "Are you deaf? Didn't you hear the name he called you?"

"Just one of his usual kindly compliments! You ought to know him by this time, my dear fellow. If he really thinks I am what he called me just now, let him prove it, let him accuse me in front of you."

Everyone present felt the contrast between his words and the somber, despairing tone in which they were uttered. And now, he, too, relapsed into silence. There were five of them on the landing, in the middle of the night, all of them more or less within sight of the truth, which only Gradère knew in its entirety. The wretched man stood there, petrified, a fixed glare in his eyes, nor did he seem to notice that each of the others was stealthily edging away. He did not hear the sound of bolts being shot. All of a sudden he gave a start. He was alone with Andrès.

"Go to bed, Papa; you're feverish."

"You're right," the other replied: "I've caught a chill. I didn't think it was anything much, but recently my temperature has been going up in the evenings."

Andrès accompanied him as far as his room, and asked him, point blank, whether he might come in for a few moments.

"I'm not well, and I'm dog-tired."

Gradère spoke in a low voice. He seemed to be pleading for a respite:

"Come and see me tomorrow morning."

"I won't stay more than a few seconds, Father, and then I'll let you get some sleep."

He followed Gradère into the room and shut the door. He glanced round him:

"This is Mamma's room…I never saw her here…I remember her only in Bilbao and Paris. Where were you when we were living in Spain?"

Gradère replied that business had kept him in France. He felt much relieved at the turn the conversation was taking.

"Your mother, my boy…only a few days ago, someone, a priest—wrote to me that she was a saint and a martyr.…"

"Why a martyr?"

Disconcerted by the question, his father answered, in his least pleasant voice, that curés always exaggerate. He gave a malicious chuckle, shrugged his shoulders, and said with sudden heat:

"Now be off with you—I'm all in!"

"Not till I know what Uncle Symphorien meant."

"You heard what he said, didn't you?" replied Gradère in bored tones. "I went to his room to talk about Cernes and Balisaou. You'll admit, I suppose, that I had a perfect right to do so? But he managed to persuade Tamati that I wanted to frighten the life out of him.… They're either mad or lying!"

"I know all about that, Papa. But the old man cried out to Tamati that she was an accessory in what happened the other night…"

Gradère was still standing, his hand on the latch. "I didn't hear that," he said at length, "you must have dreamed it."

He sauntered over to his son, his hands in his pockets.

"You know me pretty well, don't you, my boy? I don't pretend that I've lived a particularly edifying life…a bad lot, yes…but there's a whale of a difference between being a bad lot and wanting to do that old rascal in. Besides, who ever heard of anyone dying from fright? It's childish!"

Andrès drew a deep breath. The man standing there before him was no different from other men. The rest of them must be suffering from morbid imagination, and he had caught the infection.

"But you did say some pretty awful things, Papa, the other evening, about Tamati."

"If all my little jokes are going to be taken seriously! Irony is not the strong point of you people at Liogeats."

He was lolling on the sofa, looking up at Andrès:

"In Paris one can say anything—no matter how extravagant. It just goes in at one ear and out at the other. People there have got a sense of proportion. Here one's got to be answerable for the tiniest joke—it really is a bit too much! You don't understand what a joke is. That's why it is so impossible for a Parisian to live in the country! You ought to have put up a better defense: perhaps you realize now what they've got into their heads!"

Andrès was smiling, no longer tense. Gradère, too, was breathing more freely. He was once more master of the situation.

He must be careful not to let them work the boy into a state a second time. The difficulty was to arrange things so that he should hear what was said without believing what he heard.

"The game must be played out to the end."

"Old Desbats really is the limit! It's appalling what ideas a mixture of stupidity, hatred, and fright can inject into a sick man's brain! You'd scarcely credit all the talk of thieving that's going round at my expense! The comic part of the business is that the whole thing started with a dirty trick the old man played on me. I'll tell you all about it, and you can judge for yourself."

By this time he was talking fluently, relying on his gift for improvisation, and on the effect which his attitude of indulgent mockery always had on Andrès.

"I'm not exactly an angel, you know, and the old man has got on the tracks of some woman with whom I used to raise Cain in the days of my youth. She's got some letters of mine...let's leave it at that. From the purely erotic point of view, they're worth their weight in gold! Would you believe it, in order to get me out of here, they've turned to this old bitch. That nasty piece of work down the corridor actually decided to pay her ticket to Liogeats."

"But who," asked Andrès, "let the cat out of the bag?"

Gradère hesitated a moment, and then said that it had been Tamati.

"She's very fond of me, you know."

He had forgotten that only a short while ago she had been blackguarding him in Andrès' hearing. The boy, however, had not forgotten, but he said nothing.

"Well, old man, when the bitch didn't turn up on the day they were expecting her, he got it firmly fixed in his head... well, the long and the short of it is, he thinks I've killed her!"

Andrès' silence suddenly made him feel frightened. He was uneasy, and realized, at the same moment, that the boy saw that he was uneasy. He decided to brazen things out, with the result that he went rather too far. He saw that he had said more than was necessary, but lacked the presence of mind to pull up in time.

"But they were out of luck. You see, according to their reckoning, it all ought to have happened on Monday night— but on that particular night it so happened that I was safely tucked up in bed."

In a low voice, Andrès repeated the words "Monday night."

"Tamati can vouch for what I'm telling you. She spent part of the night looking after me...."

Obviously he had blundered. Once more a sort of fog had settled down between them. The boy kept from looking at him, but Gradère knew very well what the expression in his eyes would have been if he had let him see them. In that midnight silence neither father nor son could find a word to say. Andrès moved towards the door, his shoulders hunched, and this time it was Gabriel who would gladly have kept him there could they only have chatted about indifferent subjects. He called to him to come back, but in vain. The boy did not so much as turn his head.

Andrès did not go back to his room. Instead, he went down stairs and lit the hanging lamp in the hall. He gave a faint gasp. Catherine was still there.

All he said to her was:

"Not gone to bed yet?"

But he did not repel her. The load he carried was too heavy. At that moment of his destiny he would have clung to anybody, and because Catherine happened to be there, it was on her that he threw himself with a moan. She scarcely moved at all under the impact of his body. The frail slip of a girl supported the full weight of the young and stricken oak that smothered her with all its rain-drenched leaves. She took to herself part of his terrible grief. That, at least, they could share. Because together they had broken this loaf of sour bread, they would, from now on, have everything in common. They mingled their tears. But, while he, with all the strength of his being, longed for death, she, with eyes closed, and her face pressed to his body, like a baby at the breast, drank, for the first time, that hot and feverish draught, drawing life and nourishment from the broken and defeated man at her side.

18.

THE next day was the first Friday in December. As soon as Mass was over young Lassus crossed the choir, opened the door of the sacristy, and saw, at once, that the curé's Act of Grace would last too long to permit of his having a word with him before school. He walked away, therefore, and Mathilde, who had been present during the service, listened to the sound of his small clogs retreating into the distance. She, waited there, alone in the church, until the Abbé Forcas should return.

She uttered no prayer, for she was conscious of an emptiness within her, and felt hopelessly abandoned. Any appeal from her would wander aimlessly about the lime-washed vaulting, and before the altar with its load of tarnished gilt vases filled with artificial flowers. But she did not care. It was a man of whom she had come in quest, a man who would, perhaps, listen to what she had to say, would try to understand, would tell her what she ought to do. For her there was no choice—she must obey. As a human being he was young, but he was a priest. The question whether he was strong

215

enough to carry the load she was about to lay on him did not arise. Of him she could demand anything, because he was a priest, and when a man is a priest we may soil his spirit with any abomination, no matter how gross, may darken his heart with any secret, no matter how foul.

What could he be doing? She heard the heavy ticking of the clock, the crowing of a distant cock, the sawmill's scream. Outside these walls was the life of the world. It seemed to her that the church was like a dead heart within a living body. To pass the time, she went over in her mind what it was that she had come to say. She would present the matter, insofar as it concerned herself, in the best possible light. Very rarely is a woman's confession an act of accusation.

She had been waiting for nearly half an hour. Could it be that he had left without noticing her? She felt surprised that no sounds at all—no cough, no scrape of a chair, no closing of a cupboard—reached her ears. Impatiently, she rose from her knees, deliberately advanced into the choir, made a brief and perfunctory genuflection, pushed open the Sacristy door—and stopped dead.

There was nothing very strange about what she saw, nothing but a young priest on his knees after Mass. His head was inclined slightly towards the left, his eyes were closed, his hands resting, on one of those backless stools designed to keep choirboys from lolling. The room was untidy because young Lassus had not been able to put back in their places the cruets, the alb, and the chasuble. No, the scene was nothing at all out of the ordinary. Nevertheless, Mathilde had a feeling that she ought to go away, that she was prying into a secret. The humblest objects in this little country sacristy—the cruets, the metal platter, the old wash basin and tap fixed to the wall—seemed to stand out in a light that was not of this world, a light of which this rigid, motionless man was the source. It was as though a dog's distant barking, the drone of the sawmill waxing and waning with the breeze, reached her from another planet.

She heard a sigh, stepped backwards without shutting the door, and returned to her chair.

As soon as school was over, young Lassus ran to the church. A low mutter, first of one voice, then of another, warned him that the curé was taking confession. A glance at the penitent's shoes, visible beneath the curtain, led the boy to conclude that they belonged to the lady from the great house, who had been present during Mass. She had come back. How pleased the curé would be!

She showed no sign of leaving the confessional, and young Lassus began tidying up the sacristy. When he had finished there, he went back into the church. The lady was still there. What a lot of sins she must have to confess! If he went close, he might hear! But he kept as far from the confessional as he could, sat down before the altar of the Virgin, and brought from his pocket a much-knotted rosary which it took him a long time to disentangle. From his far vantage point he watched the shoes under the curtain. Every few moments, one of them moved, fidgeted slightly, and then became still. Eleven o'clock struck. His aunt would be getting anxious. He made a genuflection, smiled at the Virgin, gave one last hurried squint at the lady's shoes, and left the church with a loud clatter of clogs.

19.

WHEN Mathilde reached home, she found the house more silent than it had ever been. The events of the previous night, when all the sufferers under this roof had met, suddenly, on the very brink of a truth which all of them believed was at last to be revealed, had had no after-effects. Each one of these human entities had recoiled from the light and gone to ground in their several secrecies, there to await whatever it was that might eventually take on form and substance. Catherine and her mother had merely changed places. The young girl now filled in Andrès' life the place until then occupied by Mathilde, while the latter had replaced Catherine with old Desbats, who was in a terrible state of nerves because he had been responsible for getting Aline there and might be involved in the subsequent unpleasantness. To such an extent did Gradère feel himself to be excluded from the family circle that he could not get over the feeling that his physical presence at the chateau of Liogeats had ceased to have the slightest importance. He was free to go or stay. He had been "suppressed," and lived on now like a diseased pine tree which has been isolated from its fellows by a ditch so that it may be prevented from spreading infection, and left to die alone. Never again would he feel Andrès' eyes upon him, unskilled though the boy was in keeping them averted. Of his own accord he had taken to absenting himself from the family meals. He used his quarrel with Desbats as an excuse to board at Lacote's. He still slept at the chateau, but returned to it each evening only when he was sure that its inhabitants would be safely in their rooms.

It was now winter. Andrès, who was forever out after woodcock and hares, made longer expeditions for duck into the Teychoueyres marshes whenever the nights were suitable. He did not object to Catherine going with him. He could hardly have borne to be alone. Although they never spoke of what was in both their minds, he could not have endured the companionship of a woman ignorant of the nature of his torment. Catherine knew: like him, she was waiting. Side by side they bent over the papers (never had there been so many papers at Liogeats), their heads touching. They turned at once to the paragraphs of miscellaneous news, glanced hurriedly through them, then read them all again from the beginning.

The young girl gave expression to nothing that might have been taken for emotion. Her sole concern was to look after Andrès' material comfort, to surround him with a constant atmosphere of discreet protection. On fine Sundays he broke away from her and played practice games of football with his friends in preparation for the spring matches. Whenever he had some definite job to do—a sale to discuss, a farm to visit—she let him go alone, and it was he who, on his return after dark, called out, as soon as he got into the hall,

"Where are you, Catherine?" When that happened, she came at once to his summons. He found nothing strange in seeing her kneel down, as Tamati had done in the past, to take off his shooting-boots. If his trapper's coat had not kept him dry, she made him change his shirt. She had unquestioned access to his bedroom.

All this Mathilde noticed, and said nothing. As the winter months passed, Catherine relaxed her attitude of watchfulness. One afternoon, Andrès was riding alone along the Balisaou road. As he passed the spot known as "The Rock," he noticed a man sitting in the sunlight on the brink of an abandoned gravel pit. He reined in his horse and saw that the man was his father, and that he seemed to be busy writing on his knee. Turning round, he regained the main road.

This is what the man was writing:

What purpose can be served by my telling you about the "event"? I have no doubt that Mathilde has made full use of the permission I gave her, and that by this time you know as much as she does. Of all the actions of my life it was the least criminal, because it was so wholly in tune with my nature. Nevertheless, as I see it (strange, though it may seem) it remains the one thing I have done that is utterly unpardonable. Nothing else weighs a straw in the scale against that murder. I know perfectly well how a man of your cloth would explain this conviction of mine. The fouler the victim, you would say, the more irreparable the gesture that sent her to her death. I once knew on old priest at Luchon (I told you something else he said, do you remember?) who made use of that theory as an argument against the death penalty. Have I destroyed Aline's last hope of salvation? Was I merely an instrument in the hand of your God for the meting out of His justice? Sheer lunacy, dear reverend sir! As you see, I read your mind with perfect ease. But fortunately, there is no presence here, none at all, except that of a decomposing corpse within a few feet of me. I am writing this on my knee, sitting in the gravel pit where, forty years ago, the little Du Buch girls and the little Gradère boy had such happy times.

The sun has gone in and it is cold. Ever since I was compelled to spend two nights in this spot, I have been coughing badly. I am telling you all this because there is no one else to tell. I can no longer breathe the same air as the others. I try in vain to catch Andrès' eye. Andrès has pronounced judgment against me. I have lost him, and it was my own silly fault. I, who know so well how to deal with cunning, am like wax in the hands of young innocence. Now that I have lost him forever, nothing matters any longer. In the presence of such simplicity, one is powerless. If he ever read a book, if he ever dabbled in ideas, he would have "romanticized" the situation, would, perhaps, have developed a sense of duty towards me.... But what can one expect of a dear, brainless creature like that? His reactions are those of the man who shouts "String him up!" when he sees a condemned criminal on his way to the gallows.

Nothing has come out yet, or, at least, not in the papers. When will they make up their minds? I can't wait much longer. If they go on saying nothing, I shall summon a family council and start the ball rolling. I have often imagined the scene. It will be staged in old Desbat's bedroom. I shall tell them that I acted in self-defense, that I had no choice, that it wasn't I who brought the woman to Liogeats, that, in any case, somebody had to be a victim, so that I merely got in first. I know I could have run away as Mathilde wanted me to do. But that was only pretense on her part: actually, she was utterly dependent on me. Put baldly, she expected to find her happiness in me. Did anyone hold me back when I was already walking on the brink of crime? Did anyone so much as make a gesture? On the evening before it happened, I ran after you in the rain. But the look you turned on me had nothing in it of love (and that's putting it mildly!). In a very official, very "clergyman" voice, you said: "I am at the disposition of anyone who wishes to speak privately to me." That's not good enough, my friend. I stretched a hand to you in the darkness, and you saw fit to ignore it. You behaved as though you did not see it. I am not blaming you, you poor, childlike young man. No matter how warm your answering pressure might have been, it would still have become the hand of a criminal on the night of that Monday-Tuesday. Nothing would have been changed. Still, I do want you to think of me as I really am, without too much horror, because, well, do you remember those branches on your doorstep? It was I who cleared them away, the night I got to Liogeats (but perhaps you don't know what I am talking about).

Thank you for writing to me. I tore up the letter—I had to. I deeply regret the necessity, because although there was something slightly official, something rather formal, about it, I should like to be able to re-read it now—to try to understand it. How can I expect you to accept the fact that I believe in the Devil? You think it's just a childish pose on my part, don't you? Besides, he wouldn't want me to believe in him. What does loving God mean? An emotional impulse directed to an entity! Why, the very idea is unthinkable! Loving is an act that involves the flesh. What you are doing, my poor sir, is to transpose: you are guilty of performing, in the jargon of the day, a "transference." You—but what's the point in my going on? I know what you will say before you say it…you have put your finger into the print of the nails and thrust your hand into His side; your head has been laid upon His bosom…. What I find so curious is that a decent high-minded chap like Andrès should not have the remotest idea of an invisible world, or of that ocean whose tides flow in upon us from all sides and eat away our substance; whereas I, spattered with blood and filth as I am, have a very clear idea of what it is you do each morning in your empty church, of what it is that is accomplished there, so clear an idea, in fact, that I can even imagine your sense of inner silence, your feeling of joy….

Quietly, imperceptibly, the night was advancing into the underbrush. For a few brief moments Gradère wrote on, unable to see what he was writing. He could hear in the pines the whispering of a shower, but it was not the heavy rain which had built a screen about his crime, and he had been listening to the sound for some time before he felt the first drops upon his face. Quite unconscious of the fact that he was imitating Andrès, and with the same intention, he unbuttoned his shirt. The damp evening wind crept under his clothes. The rain began to run over the same skinny chest which, years ago, in the summer holidays, Mathilde had seen glistening with water at the pool above the lock. He felt no fear of the decomposing body nearby. It was not remorse that had drawn him to the Rock, but, perhaps, the horror of being alone. He coughed: he was feverish, and walked with difficulty. As he passed the presbytery he slipped a folded paper beneath the door. He did not much care who read it...but the Abbé had no servant. He stopped at Lacote's, drank a Pernod, and got through a bottle of wine with his meal. At the *table d'hote* three commercial travelers were discussing the advantages and disadvantages of cars in their work. They were soon deep in calculation: "But, look here, you're not taking depreciation into account...allowing for petrol at today's price...of course, wear and tear on tires is to some extent a matter of luck...." They were all speaking at once with a quite extraordinary vehemence. Gradère, who was, by this time, slightly drunk, listened to every word the men uttered, as though his life depended on the discussion. He wiped his lips, got up, and stuffed his napkin into one of the pigeonholes ranged along the wall.

From the far end of the avenue he could see lights in the chateau windows, the light of lamps shining through the darkness. Had he been a man like other men, he would have hurried towards it. Faces would have been turned to greet him; he would have pushed Andrès' hair back with his hand before stooping to kiss his forehead. He walked up the front steps with deliberate slowness, making as much noise as possible, so as to give anyone who happened to be in the hall time to get away before he crossed the threshold. The sound of hurried footsteps did, indeed, reach his ears. Someone, however, had remained behind, and appeared to be waiting for him. It was Mathilde, whose air of indifference and placidity seemed to have wiped all meaning from her ravaged face. He pretended not to have seen her, and started to go upstairs: but she called to him:

"Have you seen this?"

She was holding out a copy of a Paris newspaper, the only one he had neglected to read in the course of the last two or three days, and showed him, on the third page, a paragraph printed in reassuringly small type:

There is still no news of Aline X, the former streetwalker, who vanished, on the 25th November, from the private hotel in the Rue de la Convention, where she had been living for the past few months. She told the manageress that she would be returning next day, took no luggage with her, and did not leave an address. Nothing has been found in her room to throw any light on her mysterious disappearance, but the police state that they are in possession of clues as a result of which they are concentrating their efforts in a certain direction. Our readers will understand that, for the time being, a high degree of reserve must be maintained. The authorities are anxious to have news of a former man friend of Aline X's who left Paris some weeks prior to her disappearance. It is thought that he may be able to give useful information.

"What an extraordinary thing!" said Gradère. "Here have I been reading every paper I could lay my hands on since… well, you know what… this one in particular, and the very first time I give it a miss…"

Mathilde seemed not to have heard him. She was already moving away, but he called her back, and there was a note of anguish.

"What ought I to do? Go, I suppose…or send the police magistrate a telegram. I mustn't give the impression that I'm lying low. Won't you come down again, Mathilde?"

She leaned over the banisters and said:

"I think you're right, but it's entirely your affair. The one person who might be able to give you useful advice is the Abbé Forcas…."

She went on upstairs, and he was left alone. A continuous sound came from the Arsenal where Andrès was filling cartridges. Gradère went as far as the door. He was frightened of entering the room, but, at last, plucked up sufficient courage to do so. Catherine was sitting beside Andrès, under a lamp, knitting. With her steel-rimmed spectacles on her nose, she looked like a little old woman. Both of them stopped what they were doing.

"I'm off tomorrow morning by the six o'clock train. I hope to be back by the end of the week."

They got up.

"So long, then," muttered Andrès, and held out a flabby hand. Gabriel looked at old Gradère's needle gun hanging on the wall. Andrès followed the direction of his gaze. Habitually slow though he was at guessing other people's thoughts, he did, perhaps, on this occasion get some inkling of what was going on in his father's mind. Whether that was so or not, Gabriel most certainly had a pretty good idea of what his son was thinking, and, maybe, of what he wanted (he was one of those simple-minded persons, such as are often to be found among soldiers, who think that the obvious thing to do, when a fellow officer has been stealing or cheating at cards, is to leave a revolver conveniently lying on the table). But perhaps Gradère was just imagining this. He left the room without turning his head. How surprised he would have been, had he gone back, to find Andrès with his head on Catherine's lap sobbing.

He tiptoed across the dining room, and the hall. The front door had already been bolted for the night. It was not cold, and there was no frost. But Gradère had neglected to take his overcoat. A patch of sky, light by comparison with the black walls made by the trees, showed him his way. He walked towards the town, where a single light was showing. It came from the Abbé's house. "He has found my letter. He can't very well *not* be thinking about me." Should he use the knocker? If he did, a window would be opened on the first floor, and a voice would ask who was there. What reply could he make? What reason to offer for this nocturnal visit which had been suggested by Mathilde? Say that he had come for advice? But he knew very well what advice a man like the Abbé would give: "Hand yourself over to justice, take your punishment, put yourself in the hands of God."

He shivered and sat down on the steps whose worn surface was already familiar to his hands. He touched them as though he were stroking an old face. He coughed, but one of the lessons he had learned in his seminary days was that no one can make himself ill of set intent. At that period of his life, he had committed the wildest imprudences with the sole object of getting the infirmary Sisters to spoil him. But never once had he managed to catch anything, whereas his attack of pleurisy had been the result of one short walk in the rain. Crouching against the door he let his mind wander among the most ordinary thoughts before making his entry on the stage and facing the music. But he did not really believe that he ever would face the music, and that was why he remained calm. He was like a seemingly cornered man who knows that at his back there lies a vast and secret countryside, rich in lines of retreat. Not that he gave serious thought to Andrès' unspoken suggestion (or what he had taken for such). Nothing would have induced him to clench his teeth on a revolver barrel and pull the trigger, nothing. Somehow or other he *would* get out of the prison of his life, *would* break the line of his destiny, *would* escape from that appalling logic of events, that combination of motives and actions, which, after fifty years, had led him back to the Rock, to the sandy playground of his childhood, one dark night with Aline. His cough sounded strangely in the peacefulness of the winter's night. But at Liogeats what night is ever wholly silent? The lightest breeze is caught by a thousand murmuring pines (as though somewhere there is always a sleeping God): the Balion gives back the sound of an unceasing ripple as it breaks against stones on which a prehistoric ocean has left the mark of shells and membranes....

A window was opened and a voice said: "Who's that coughing?" (What he had been expecting for the last hour had come!) He gave a start, but made no answer. From behind the door came the sound of hurrying steps, first on the stairs, then on the flags of the passage. Gradère had not fainted, nor did he ape unconsciousness. He remained where he was, like an inanimate object, silent, sightless, immobile—a mere stone—even when the light of a lamp fell upon his face. Two hands seized him under the arms. He could scarcely have stood unaided.

The Abbé opened a door on the left—the door of the kitchen. He made Gradère sit in a wicker armchair, and threw a handful of twigs on the ashes of the fire. He touched his visitor's forehead, then his neck.

"You can't go back to the chateau at this time of night. I'll make you up a bed."

Gradère was alone in the dead kitchen. The fire had already collapsed. On the table beneath the lamp stood some cold boiled potatoes in a soup-plate, an empty tin of sardines, and a hunk of bread.

The Abbé came back. He begged him to wait a little, because the sheets were still slightly damp. He filled a jug with hot water, and again went out.

"Now…" he said.

He helped Gradère to his feet, but the sick man moved quickly and needed no support. There was a smell of stables. The room into which he was shown was huge and fairly comfortable. It contained a carpet, a mirror hanging between the two windows, a mahogany chest of drawers, a winged armchair, a clock under a glass dome, and two candlesticks. All the Abbé's worldly possessions had been collected together into this one room. While Gradère was hastily undressing, he caught a whiff of scent. This must be where the man's sister had slept! He stretched himself between the sheets and thrust his feet against the earthenware hot-water bottle. What bliss! Whoever would think of looking for him here? What human power could snatch him from this priest who was now his surety? But wasn't he due to leave the next morning by the six o'clock train? Should he telegraph to the police magistrate? He looked at the Abbé's face, which was in shadow, but could not read its expression. He tried to say something, but became entangled in his words. He realized that the other would think him delirious, and redoubled his efforts. The Abbé interrupted him. He said that he had met Madame Desbats that afternoon, and had read what was printed in the paper. He spoke reassuringly. His advice was that Gradère should write a letter. If necessary, he would add a few lines himself. No doubt a judicial commission of inquiry would be sent down to question him. His presence in the presbytery could easily be explained as the result of his quarrel with Desbats. "I don't want to be the cause of your having to tell lies." It was not difficult for the criminal in the bed to realize the scruples which, he imagined, his simple-minded host must be feeling. The Abbé gave a shrug. "As soon as it's light I'll go and see Clairac. We'll tell him the same story—that because of a family quarrel you have been compelled to lodge with me."

It was Alain who took every decision, as though he had foreseen precisely this situation, and had devoted many days to thinking about it. Standing well away from the sick man, who was already showing signs of drowsiness, he studied him carefully.

He thought to himself: "I did not know that I was waiting for him." Then, he came nearer, successfully fought down his feeling of repulsion, and looked at the hot, feverish face.

Nothing that had happened in the man's life had been able to change by a jot the purity of the original design, the clean lines of forehead, nose and mouth. Neither time nor evil-doing had debased the indestructible geography of that face. He lies there just precisely as you handed him over to me. Once I repulsed him, now I have taken him in. I could do no other than take him in. Every fresh disaster that the presence of the man beneath his roof threatened to let loose upon him, Alain had accepted in advance, not trying, even, to guess at its nature. He must act as circumstances should dictate, blindly. He lowered the shade of the lamp, took his rosary, lost himself in meditation, and fell asleep.

In the middle of the night Gradère awoke. It was borne in upon him that for some minutes, some hours, perhaps, he had been conscious of a faint grunting. The head of his sick-nurse was moving restlessly against the back of his chair. He, for his own part, felt cooler, and in better fettle than he had been for a long time. He could not remember that he had ever known such peace of mind. He glanced towards the window, and was reassured. No sign of light announced the coming day. This blessed night had still some distance to go. The wind had dropped, and the tormented treetops no longer moaned under the winter stars. It was that hour, just before the dawn, of which the majority of men know nothing.

Gradère's eyes were fixed upon the sleeping Alain, and a strange and very powerful feeling came to him. He had the illusion that the young priest in the chair was himself, that, in some other life, he had *been* this young man in black with the rather stocky body and the worn face. In another life? Or in Somebody's mind? As, by the light of the lamp, he watched with an urgent tenderness this double of himself, his attention was caught and held by the animal grunting of the sleeping man. He noted the hanging lower jaw, the thick, prominent lip which looked almost as though it were bleeding. The soul had withdrawn from the sightless face. No longer did the light that came from a fundamental purity illumine from within the animal exterior. "He might have been me." Alain might have yielded to his sister's influence, might have chosen the way of surrender, might have become the slave of obscure desires. Desires which had filled him with horror when, as a child, he had become aware of their existence.... But he might, very easily, have overcome that horror, as Gradère had done. He might have grown used to the hidden monsters in his heart, might have tamed, flattered, fed, gorged them, and more than satisfied their cravings.

The Abbé awoke with a start. Gradère closed his eyes and felt a hand upon his forehead. Then he heard a muffled sound upon the floor. Alain had knelt down and was reading his breviary. After a fairly long time, he laid it down upon the bedside table, and very quietly left the room. Gradère raised himself on his pillows, took up the black book, opened it at random, and came upon a reproduction of Rembrandt's *Christ and the Travelers to Emmaus*. On the back was written:

In memory of my ordination, 3rd June, 1922. Alain Forcas, priest. Thou shalt walk before the Lord to give knowledge of Salvation unto His People, of the remission of sins, of the tenderness of His mercy, bringing light to them that sit in darkness and in the shadow of death, to guide their feet into the way of peace.

Gabriel put the breviary back upon the table, and lay down in a state of calm lucidity. From the depths of his crime he looked up and saw this destiny as the very antipodes of his own, yet so close to him. *He* might have had the power to absolve, to lighten and to deliver, while yet remaining the same Gabriel Gradère. The one poor merit of which a man may, before God, avail himself, is that of having accepted the burden of being chosen—at least if he belongs to that race of men in whose eyes the things of this world are an unending delight. We have but one life. Gradère might, perhaps, be forgiven, but never again would he be the child who once had waked on summer mornings of holiday, and taken off his shoes and stockings the better to feel the warm sand under his feet, and stood in the stream, letting the water of the Balion eddy and divide about the dark columns of his legs. He had passed forever that milestone on his road where those who are called by name must rise and leave all that is theirs.

20.

"WELL," said Mathilde as she walked up the front steps, "everything went off splendidly...."

They were standing, all three of them, by the front door, Catherine, Andrès, and old Desbats, made one by a shared feeling of tense anxiety, and eagerly waiting to hear what she would say. But for a while she said nothing more. She drank in the air, and, for a few moments, closed her eyes. It had been raining. Cockchafers were booming, and a wind from the east had touched all the lilacs of the little town.

"So far as I could gather from the curé, who was present at each occasion of the Commission's sittings, the magistrate treated Gradère as a very sick man, and never seems seriously to have suspected him for a moment...." She broke off, and glanced round her uneasily.

"Let's not stay out here...."

When they were all ensconced in the Arsenal, she began again, speaking very quietly:

"The police have no idea at all where the woman went to. Because, when she left Paris, Gradère was already established here with the family, no notice has been taken of the anonymous letter which indicated, in the vaguest terms, that he was the guilty party. Furthermore"—with a glance at her husband—"they have been able to piece together two letters (unsigned and without envelopes), both of them typewritten, to which a postscript had been added: *Whatever you do, write nothing that might arouse G.'s suspicions. He would most certainly find some way to prevent you from coming.* This was interpreted in Gradère's favor. The magistrate is quite convinced that the murderer is the man who wrote those letters."

"But in that case," broke in Desbats in a frightened voice, "I might be accused...."

Catherine put her arm round his neck.

"Poor, dear Papa," she said, "you're crazy!"

Mathilde did her best to reassure him:

"Gradère," she went on, "made an excellent impression by saying that he had long been out of touch with the circles in which Aline moved; that for years he had had nothing to do with her except to help her occasionally with money. Actually, they have found a number of cheque counterfoils, as well as an account book, which go to prove how generous he was to her."

Desbats, struggling for breath, said again:

"They'll say it was I...I shall be charged..."

He had a fit of choking. Catherine had brought down everything needed for an injection. He was, by this time, beyond speech, but his eyes never left his wife's lips. She continued with her efforts to reassure him:

"But I've told you already, they are closing the inquiry. The magistrate has left for Bazas, and there will be no further questioning.... Besides, Gradère is in a very bad way. Clairac is of the opinion that the other lung is affected, and that the progress of the disease will be very rapid. It is too late to try a pneumothoracic operation. The end might be delayed if he were willing to go to Switzerland, but he won't hear of leaving the presbytery. Fortunately, the Abbé is prepared to keep him there. Really, for the last four months, while all this has been going on, our poor little curé has been magnificent. It's no fun to have a sick man like that on the premises...and, at his age, there is considerable risk of infection."

Desbats recovered sufficient breath to say that the curé knew perfectly well that they wouldn't let him be the loser, and that he stood to get a substantial sum of money. Still, there was no getting away from it: he *had* done the family a great service. Mathilde smiled, shrugged, and, turning to Andrès, remarked:

"Ever since he took a turn for the worst, the Abbé has been sitting up with him every other night. Young Lassus' aunt relieves him.... But he really is at the end of his tether. I told him that you would lend a hand tonight. He'll be expecting you about eleven."

Andrès growled something about having more than once offered to help, but that the sick man had refused to see him.

"Yes, from a sense of shame. But since this morning your father has become resigned to the idea of meeting you. He's a totally different man. He has changed quite unbelievably. He even wanted to give himself up to the police. It was only with the greatest difficulty that the Abbé kept him from doing so. He only managed it at last by talking to him of you, Andrès."

Desbats, who had got up and was now clinging to Catherine's arm, turned round at this and said with malicious emphasis:

"You're not going to be taken in by that, I hope! He's got more than one trick up his sleeve! I shan't know a moment's peace until…"

Mathilde motioned to Andrès not to say anything. When they were alone, she remarked in a colorless voice:

"I'm going up to your uncle's room to take over from Catherine. Go outside and wait for her to come down."

Andrès took an overcoat and sat on the front steps. He could hear the frogs and the fluttering of wings in the drenched lilacs.

Over towards Frontenac, two nightingales were calling to one another in notes of melancholy tenderness. But he took notice of these things only insofar as they gave him information about the time of day, the season of the year, and the likelihood of it being fine on the morrow. All that interested him in the sky was the direction in which the clouds were moving.

He felt very tranquil. His criminal father was at the point of death. He would marry Catherine. Once again, life was becoming simple and normal. At last he was freed from the agony that had been lying so heavy upon him for the last four months. He had no right to raise difficulties. He had detached himself from, had utterly renounced, everything that he had wanted in the days before this crime, everything that, directly or indirectly, was associated in his mind with the memory of his father. He wanted never again to hear talk of love or of any silliness of that kind. He would live, he would have children, he would be rich, and then, what? Every now and again he would go into Bordeaux for a spree. Provided, always, that there were no complications, that no letter turned up, that no witnesses appeared unexpectedly.

And what about the body? He had put that question, one evening, to Tamati.

"I know nothing," she had stammered in reply, "except that it can't be found...."

Anyhow, his father would cheat justice by conveniently dying.

He heard Catherine hurrying down the stairs. She was breathing heavily.

"Let's go for a walk, dear, shall we?"

She took him off. In her absence he had nothing for her but feelings of friendship and gratitude. But when she was with him, she got on his nerves. He resented especially the hunger for him which she found it so impossible to disguise. This evening, she, too, seemed as though a great weight had been lifted from her shoulders. If only this storm would move away! It was her turn now to know happiness. She had certainly paid heavily enough for it in advance! Pressed close to Andrès, she walked by the Frontenac meadows. Far off, the two nightingales were still calling. Because of the distance, the purity of their notes sounded unreal.

"How clear the sky is—look!" she exclaimed.

With a bored air Andrès raised his eyes and saw, through a gap in the branches, an expanse of rain-washed blue.

"What of it?" he asked.

"Let's sit down on this bench."

She buried her face in his shoulder and did not move. He tried not to see her.

"I'm going to sit up with my father tonight. I only hope he doesn't say anything."

She begged him not to think about that man. It was all over now, the whole wretched business.

"I am so happy."

He felt her cold lips on his neck, and his body suddenly remembered Tota. There came an uprush of feeling for the woman he had lost. No sooner had the danger in which his father was involved been swept aside, than the other pain came back, the pain that really mattered, his secret poison, the love without which life would be impossible. What was he doing on this bench? At the mercy of this female creature's skinny little hands, of this praying mantis? He dared not move, fearful lest he compromise himself. He sat on, aping death.

Catherine knew perfectly well that he had no feeling for her, that he was a corpse. But in that corpse lay all her satisfaction. She held between her arms the adored being whose thoughts, the while, were far away. She had, at least, his body, and that was better than nothing. With the tips of her fingers, and as though absentmindedly (but really with what concentration!) she just touched the down that covered the coarse hand.

He was feeling all that Tota would have felt at this moment. He heard, as she would have heard, the nightingales singing in the Frontenac woods. They were so far away that their call seemed to come from some unknown world. He saw, with Tota's eyes, through the black tracery of the branches, a faintly muted azure, a sky poor in stars, as though the constellations had not yet been created. It had the fresh look of Eden in its infancy, after the ending of the primal chaos. All that he was incapable of imagining for himself, he knew through the medium of Tota, so strong was her presence in him. Yet, at the same time, he was Andrès, a youth of twenty-two, half peasant, little more than a brute beast. He would break through every obstacle and go to her without asking permission of the little curé. He needed nobody now. All the same, he must be careful in his dealings with Catherine, and marry her without further delay. Once that was done....

The girl, her head on Andrès' breast, could feel the faintly quickened beating of his heart. But she had no presentiment of tragedy. Suddenly, with a sigh, he pushed her from him, though not roughly, and seemed to be listening. She looked at him uneasily. In a low voice (as though he were hearing them for the first time in his life) he said:

"The nightingales...."

Mathilde, too, heard them, though the windows of Symphorien's room were shut. Lying there in a haze of smoke from his herbal cigarettes, the upper part of his body supported on pillows, he had fallen asleep. But even in sleep, terror had fast hold of him.

Every now and again he gave vent to groans and protestations of innocence. She drew aside the curtains and pressed her face to the glass. She could hear the sound made by the Balion as it dashed over its stony bed, and, from over Frontenac way, the plaint of the two birds. Symphorien had told her not on any account to open the casement "because of all the pollen and muck" that made his crises worse. But she felt unable to breathe in the fetid atmosphere of the room. The mingled smell of cigarette smoke and urine had an asphyxiating effect on her. Only a thin pane of glass stood between her and the freshness of the night air, between her and the milky whiteness of the foaming stream, the rustling darkness that lay upon the late lilac and the early hawthorn. Her fingers touched the latch, but she withdrew them.

She had changed her mind. The Abbé had said to her, "Do not worry yourself about the part you played in this crime. You are absolved from all guilt, of that I can assure you, but on condition that you accept, from now on, the duty of attending to your husband's every want. God asks of you complete acquiescence, unconditional surrender." At first obedience to this injunction had brought her only peace and happiness. But this evening, for the first time since her confession, she had felt that she could bear no more.

She was conscious of feeling strangely alive and strangely free. Was it because human justice had withdrawn from Gradère, because the shadow of death that lay already upon the criminal was about to swallow up the whole squalid tale? Now that the blood was flowing with renewed vigor through her veins, why should she be bound to a man who was already half dead, whose very sleep bore the imprint of mortality. The others had lost no time. They were picking up again the clue of their happiness: yes, Andrès and Catherine...Andrès and Catherine.

At this very moment they were walking in the darkness, were together, were united. She let the curtain fall and slipped into her dressing room. Its only source of light was an attic window. In order to get a breath of the night air she climbed on to a stool on which stood a pile of bound copies of

Illustration which served to distract Symphorien when sleep would not come. She stretched her head out into the glimmering, the branchy and star-filled darkness. She felt upon her face the coolness of the damp air. From the croaking Frontenac meadows came the smell of growing waterplants. The wind had changed and was no longer heavy with the scent of lilac. The heavy woman grotesquely perched upon a scaffolding of books, her elbows scraped by the roof tiles, took her fill of the perfumed, rain-washed, darkness. She was just a woman now, with all a woman's longings.

"Mathilde!"

The volumes of *Illustration* collapsed. The breathless voice went on:

"Something tells me you have opened the attic window."

She went back into the room, protesting her innocence.

"I haven't, really I haven't. I knocked over the stool by mistake, that's all. Go to sleep. I'm going to bed, too."

She laid her hand upon the bald, perspiring forehead. So acrid was the air of the room that she held her breath. By a supreme effort of the will, she forced herself to pray, knowing full well that she would find no message, no comfort, in words learned by rote, words which did not come from her heart. She prayed, though she belonged to that race of dead souls who never hear God's answer. She prayed, conscious of nothing but the wheezing of asthmatic lungs, and, far away, in spite of the closed windows, from beyond the meadows, the sound of the stream punctuated by the song of the two nightingales. It ceased, perhaps because the two birds had found one another at last, and nothing broke the silence but the gurgling of swift water flowing beneath the alders.

The door was opened noiselessly (as only Catherine knew how to open it). Mathilde saw the girl's shadowy form slip into the room.

"Wouldn't you like a breath of fresh air, Mamma? Andrès has gone across to the presbytery. He'll be watching there till dawn. Stay out as long as you want to. It's a marvelous night."

Mathilde got up. She could not see her daughter's face, but she had only to hear the girl speak to know that she was happy, that she was experiencing that unexpected bliss of those who know that all life's riches are theirs. She thanked her in a flat voice, saying that, yes, a little air would do her good.

The moon was rising. Instead of following the main avenue, Mathilde turned into a path whose sandy surface seemed whiter in the darkness than it did in daylight, and stopped without a moment's hesitation in front of a certain pine tree, the very tree which, thirty years before, had formed the back wall of the hut, the "jouquet." It had not changed. On its huge trunk the gashes of that earlier time showed now as ancient scars. She who once had been a young girl, now leaned her withered cheek against it. With her forehead pressed to the bark, her eyes shut, drunk with memories and broken by life, she saw in the backward of her childhood the glimmer of the boy Gradère's blue eye. Figures pressed in upon her: Adila, the servant of the poor and ailing, who also had been a wild young madcap; Andrès, the beloved young animal; a woman known as Tota, another called Aline, and the priest.... At last courage was given her to look with steady gaze upon the terror that had grown, through fifty years, in this small corner of the world, between these creatures of a day, beneath the everlasting eyes. It would continue still, in Andrès, in Catherine, in the children who would spring from them…and in her, too, for she must drain to the dregs an old age that might well be interminable (but her desire, never would *that* be drained!)—an unknown sequence of long, tormenting years.

Death would not cry halt to what the dead had started. Gabriel might disappear—since it is the law of life that poison shall outlive the reptile who has carried it. But from whom had that other Gradère, the small boy with the blue eyes, received the dreadful heritage? Where shall we find our beginnings? What growing reeds must we push aside to discover the source of the tainted stream?

And yet another power, she did not doubt it, existed somewhere. Adila had been saved: the young and criminal creature who had corrupted her was already more than halfway to eternity. Even at Liogeats the hope that lives in human hearts had won its victory. Love had conquered, the love whose true lineaments are hidden from the eyes of this world.… Though from it she had never received any apparent aid, though it had given her no answer, she would press towards it blindly, believing in the light, with praying hands outstretched—because of the grace that had been granted her, because once her eyes had gazed upon a man who spoke with God in the shabby Liogeats presbytery. But it was not for herself that Mathilde sought salvation, nor with a mind dwelling on her own eternity, for what lay beyond the life of the body she could not grasp in thought. True to her womanhood, she was drawn by every fiber back to Andrès. Of the faith that had been rekindled in her heart to a flicker of uncertain flames, she treasured, first and foremost, the power it gave her to suffer for another. If only it could bring some happiness to the child she loved so well, then gladly would she consent to live and die in the squalor of that fetid room.

"IT is time I went to sit with my father," Andrès had said.

He knew that the Abbé Forcas would not be expecting him before eleven, but he could no longer bear the feel of Catherine's head upon his shoulder. She had suggested going with him as far as the first houses of the town, and he could think of no excuse turned aside to contemplate another aspect of existence, to look at the face that life showed in the throbbing darkness. He was being assailed by the scented dark and the sappy odors of the earth. Within that room a man lay dying who had never ceased to keep faith with the flesh, obedient to its every demand, so wholly subservient to its will that he had even committed crime in its name. Yet he was sleeping now in the arms of God. "Peace has come to him at the end," thought Alain. "But oh, my God! I have, since the beginning, agreed that You alone should live in my heart. I have shared You with nobody, and all that this darkness brings I would strangle without regret as often as might be necessary, because it is You I love."

AT the sound of the door opening he turned his head and saw Andrès. Moving from the window, he shook hands with the young man who stood there, taking in the appearance of the room—not of the bed on which his father lay dozing, but of the room which he knew had once been Tota's. The priest realized at once that she was uppermost in Andrès' mind, and a rancorous anger began to rise in him, a feeling of hatred which he recognized for what it was, for he had long been used to keeping a careful watch upon himself. At once he bent the whole power of his will to keep in subjection this savage uprush of emotion. He did his best to smile, to answer the questions which the young man was putting to him in a low voice.

But deep inside him insidious words were forming: "See what delight he feels at being within these four walls. His father matters nothing to him. It is of her that he is thinking, of Tota…nor need he fall back upon conjectures. Nobody has known her better than he—nobody!"

"How pale you are!" said Andrès. "Are you sure that you're feeling all right?"

The Abbé shook his head without replying. He was clenching his teeth. He muttered something about needing air, and, while Andrès took his place beside the bed, went back to the window. The nightingales were now asleep, the poplars had ceased their rustling. "Did I yield to my impulse of hatred?" he asked himself in an access of mental torment: "Am I still in a state of grace?" Would he be able, in a few hours' time, to say his Mass? "Well," murmured that same voice of the tempter, "why not refrain from going to the altar tomorrow morning? Where there is the slightest doubt." But what reason for his defection could he give young Lassus? No longer seeing his way plain before him, Alain clung to a rule that he had made his own: to surrender to a very lunacy of trust, to be trusting even to the brink of lunacy. But what of sacrilege? The memory that he could never silence brought to his mind a fragment of the

Gospel: *Friend, how is it that you came in here without having a wedding garment? And the servants took him and cast him into outer darkness.*

But now the sick man had awakened, and was speaking in a low voice to Andrès. The Abbé, from the depths of his temptation, lost not a word of what they were saying. "I am dying in peace, dear Andrès," Gradère repeated more than once, "in a peace beyond imagining." Then, in Alain's heart, the old grievance rose again. He had been cheated, robbed! What mockery, what derision! This criminal would be saved, but he…he was lost. And yet, in spite of the stormy surface of his spirit, another voice, muted by distance, made itself heard within his heart across a great chasm of misery: "I am there, fear not. I am there forever."

The young priest's head was damp with sweat. He leaned it against the cross-piece of the window-frame. (How often during his nights of vigil had he gazed with adoration at this cross made by the window against the blackness of the night!) On his forehead he could feel the bruise made by the great nail, and, on his hair, the warm blood trickling from the sacred feet. For such a baptism was he born. He felt suffocated by love. He closed his eyes.

Gradère called to him. He gave a start and went across to the bed. Andrès, his head turned away, was standing a little apart.

"What in the world is there that I can give you in exchange for all that you have given me. The boy has pledged me his word…you know what I am talking about, don't you? You need not fear him any longer. That's so, isn't it, Andrès? Tell him yourself."

The young man made a sign of assent, but he did not turn round. Deep silence filled the room.

"I'll sit with him for the rest of the night," said the Abbé. "I'm used to it. You go to bed."

Andrès got up and kissed his father on the forehead. Alain went downstairs with him and drew the bolt of the front door. On the worn steps, every wrinkle of which stood out clearly in the moonlight, they stood facing one another. At that moment a simple look, a pressure of the hand, was enough to express the regard that the two men felt for one another.

CLUNY MEDIA

Designed by Fiona Cecile Clarke, the CLUNY MEDIA *logo
depicts a monk at work in the scriptorium,
with a cat sitting at his feet.*

*The monk represents our mission to emulate
the invaluable contributions of the monks
of Cluny in preserving the libraries of the West,
our strivings to know and love the truth.*

*The cat at the monk's feet is Pangur Bán, from the
eponymous Irish poem of the 9th century.
The anonymous poet compares his scholarly
pursuit of truth with the cat's happy hunting of mice.
The depiction of Pangur Bán is an homage to the work
of the monks of Irish monasteries and a sign
of the joy we at Cluny take in our trade.*

"Messe ocus Pangur Bán,
cechtar nathar fria saindan:
bíth a menmasam fri seilgg,
mu memna céin im saincheirdd."

Made in United States
Orlando, FL
28 June 2022

19244071R00143